THE VEIL
OF
MAPLES AND PINES

Steve Leadley

A Beach Reeds publication

Look for other books by Steve Leadley at:

www.steveleadleyauthorpage.weebly.com

ISBN: 978-0-9800944-4-2

Library of Congress Cataloging-in-Publication Data
Leadley, Steve
The Veil of Maples and Pines/ Steve Leadley
Beach Reeds, 2013

Historical Fiction/Antebellum South/Slavery/Coming
of Age/Historical Mystery

FOREWORD

The racial pejoratives and prejudices that litter this story are an unwelcome necessity for maintaining historical accuracy. Likewise, the stilted colloquial speech of the slaves is not meant as a slight to those unfortunate souls kept in involuntary servitude, but again to preserve that authenticity of the atmosphere of the antebellum South.

CHAPTER 1

Murder. When someone commits murder they do so for a reason. The motivations are almost limitless, I suppose. Whether murder is ever warranted, is up for debate. I mean taking someone's life seems harsh payment for any offense. "Murder." It truly is a dirty word. It is punishable by death in its own right. More murder.

Killing in warfare is not murder, or so we have been told. In battle killing is not only accepted, but encouraged. A soldier has not been personally wronged by his opponent, yet he has marked him for death. It is intriguing that murder, even in retribution for some wretched action is considered heinous, and yet killing a man whom you've never met, who's never done anything to you, is cause for praise.

I imagine that General Grant will be rewarded for all the death he has caused. Our unit has been here at Vicksburg since the end of December. We encountered harsh fighting a day ago (May 19) and are currently tending to our wounded. We lost twenty-five men yesterday.

The city is holding, but food is becoming scare, and it's not just the army that is suffering, but the folk of Vicksburg as well. Most have moved to the caves for protection from the artillery, but the hillside can't save them from starvation.

General Pemberton was given the task of protecting Vicksburg not because of his abilities, but because of his friendship with Jeff Davis. Davis may be the President of the Confederacy, but he should never have allowed friendship to interfere with his military appointments. I mean Pemberton is not even a southerner! He is from Pennsylvania, I think. Pemberton is obviously becoming desperate as he awaits relief from General Johnston. Johnston has been expected since the siege began, and if he arrives, the situation may reverse itself.

Vicksburg is the most brutal fighting I've seen thus far. The final battle for the city will likely occur on the 22nd and since I am not altogether confident that I will survive, I think it prudent that I relate the peculiar events that caused me to act in the manner that so perplexed and angered my friends and neighbors.

I cannot assure the reader that my recollections are completely without embellishment or ornamentation since I am writing of events that occurred a decade ago. However, I pledge to give as accurate an account as I am able.

I suppose for my story to make sense I shall have to start with my own beginnings. My name is Gideon Covington. I was born in Botetourt County Virginia in March of 1837. My father, James Covington was killed in action during the war with Mexico. My mother, Elizabeth remarried in 1848, two years after my Father's death. She wed my father's younger brother Robert who had been widowed a year earlier. My uncle, mother, I, and my uncle's two daughters from his first marriage, Ellen and Eliza all lived on the Covington family plantation "The Copper Beeches."

At our plantation we had about 450 acres of farmland, and 14 slaves. The Copper Beeches had been in our family for generations. Though many of the inhabitants of the Shenandoah Valley were descendants of the German and Scotch-Irish that settled the valley in the 1730's and 40's, we were of English stock. My great-grandfather had moved from the tidewater region after the French and Indian War to begin planting tobacco. The land passed to my grandfather, father, and then on to Uncle Robert and finally to me.

Plantations are not plentiful in the valley, and our place was of only moderate size compared to those in eastern Virginia. Our neighbor Colonel Jeffers's plantation, "Chiltern Grange," is more in line with those of the eastern part of the state, or at least

2

he tries to pretend that it is. It seems the planters in the east hold a degree of contempt for those of us farther west. People like ourselves and the Jeffers might not be welcome into the gentry of our eastern brethren, but we were certainly among the elite in our less hospitable area of the state.

Life was good at The Copper Beeches and my uncle was a good man. He was very kind, though a bit aloof at times. My mother was an erudite woman and insisted that her children be educated. Ellen, and Eliza and I, all took daily lessons from Mother. I was an extremely studious lad, considered by some to be a genius. My intellect stood out in our rural locale, and I often lamented not living in Richmond or some such place where I could get a more thorough education. Of course, men like Ben Franklin and our own General Washington seemed to make out all right without any "formal" learning, so I soothed my conscience by believing that I could prosper as well. My two cousins were six and four years younger than I respectively, and this fact coupled with their gender and aversion to learning resulted in their not spending nearly as much time at the books as I did.

Mother treated my cousins as if they were her own, so we all received the same upbringing. My mother was stern, yet loving and fair. I know she missed my father, as did I, but Uncle Robert was a fine man, and in retrospect I can see the benefit of her accepting his proposal. I know he adored her, but the marriage also gave him a mother for his girls, and kept The Copper Beeches strictly in Covington hands. Had he married another, particularly a woman with children, there could have been rivalry and infighting as occurred in the case of Mr. MacLaren whose farm was not twenty miles away.

I have observed that memories clutter the brain in a sort of collage. It seems that major events act as markers for us to arrange our recollections in some sort of chronology. For me, the political events in the spring of 1850 serve as one such marker. I clearly recall Uncle Robert, Colonel Jeffers, and Mr. Janus sitting on our front porch discussing the debate surrounding the entrance of California into the Union.

"Have you seen the text of Calhoun's speech?" Colonel Jeffers asked. Clearly he was addressing my uncle since Mr. Janus was illiterate.

"Yes, Yes." my uncle replied with his characteristic devilish smirk. "But the honorable Mr. Calhoun is a sick man. He has not been privy to the last four months of debate in the Senate... He was even too ill to deliver the speech himself."

"Confound it, sir!" Jeffers blustered, banging the arm of his chair. "Do you not recall that I fought under General Taylor? That I fought the Mexicans for the very land in question?" My uncle's grin remained during the tirade he had intentionally provoked, but it quickly receded as Jeffers continued, "Sir, do you forget that your own brother lost his life in that conflict?"

Mr. Janus shifted uncomfortably in his chair. He desperately wanted to participate in the discussion, but was uneasy at his lack of first-hand information. Finally he thumped the table, interjecting: "Slaves should be allowed in California!" Quite pleased with his participation, he contentedly reclined in his chair.

It was no secret that Colonel Jeffers looked down upon Mr. Janus since he did not belong to what passed for the elite class in Botetourt County. Yet, the Colonel often pontificated on the virtue of republican values and thus wanted to have as many landowners as possible corroborate his ideals, even if their plot was a tiny one. Intent on "educating" Mr. Janus to the situation, he looked directly at him and said, "Henry, John C. Calhoun may not be a Virginian like us, but he speaks for the whole South on this issue. The honorable Mr. Calhoun demands that slavery be permitted in *all* of the territory we acquired from Mexico, or the South should withdraw from the Union."

4

My uncle's sorrow quickly dissipated as he scampishly jibed the Colonel once more. "You know, Henry Clay has proposed yet another compromise. He wants California to enter as a free state, the Utah and New Mexico territories to vote on the slave issue, and to prohibit the selling of slaves in Washington City. It's said that Senator Webster is going to support Clay's plan."

"Webster! That scoundrel? He wants to ban slavery from the territories altogether! You forget sir, that Henry Clay also proposes a more stringent fugitive slave law. Mr. Clay may mean well, sir, but it is Mr. Calhoun who represents the South. That damned Webster and his abolitionist cronies are intent on destroying our way of life! I mean he's from Massachusetts for God's sake!"

Mr. Janus was a bit lost by the political rhetoric, but he understood the premise. The abolitionists had declared war on the Southern lifestyle, and though his holdings were small, and he had to work alongside his slaves in the field, he was a Virginian and proud of it. Hell, even men that *didn't own slaves* resented the Yankee attacks on our society. "Well," Janus said uneasily, "the federal government should not be able to prevent a man from owning property."

"Yes, sir!" The Colonel banged the arm of his chair once again. "Yes, indeed! That is the crux of the matter. Our property rights are under attack. Further, a state should be allowed to govern itself without interference from outside. Why in the world should I allow some Yankee from up yonder to tell me how to live my life? That, sir, is exactly Mr. Calhoun's point. It is a state's right to decide for itself!"

The vote of affirmation greatly contented Mr. Janus. His back straightened with confidence as he smugly nodded his head in agreement.

During this conversation I sat on the steps of the porch, transfixed by the discourse. I was a mature lad and enjoyed listening to, and learning from, adults. I already knew that

Henry Clay had authored the Missouri Compromise thirty years prior, which had allowed Missouri to enter the Union as a slave state, and Maine as a free state. The Compromise had also divided the west at thirty-six degrees thirty minutes' latitude with slavery being permitted below that line. At that time the issue was the balance of the Senate; trying to keep equal the number of slave and free states. *This* however was a different matter. During the last decade, the abolitionists had begun to gain ground in national politics, and the Southern way of life was now under attack.

It was about this time that Mother came out of the house and stood quietly behind the men until Colonel Jeffers had finished his acceptance of Mr. Janus' opinions.

"Excuse me gentlemen, will you be staying for supper?" she asked.

The question alerted the men to her presence and they immediately stood, respectfully removing their hats.

"I'm sorry ma'am, I didn't know you were there..." the Colonel blushed at his apparent discourtesy.

My uncle's wry grin betrayed that he was reflecting on the ire the Colonel must have felt at my mother equating Mr. Janus to himself by referring to both as "gentlemen."

"No, No, thank you ma'am," Janus stammered, "I really must be gittin' on home." Mr. Janus looked down deferentially, as he shook hands with my uncle and the Colonel before skulking off the porch.

"Thank you kindly ma'am," the Colonel continued, "but I am sure Mrs. Jeffers will be expecting me."

"Are you sure? I can have Covey set another place?" Mother replied.

"You're too kind, ma'am, perhaps another time."

With that Uncle Robert let loose a loud whistle and out of nowhere appeared Jeremy, one of the field hands. "Fetch the Colonel's horse, Jeremy."

6

"Yas sir, Massa." And quick as a flash, the slave was back with "Champion" the Colonel's prized stallion.

The Colonel mounted, removed his hat once again and bowed; elegantly flourishing the hat before him. Without another word he rode off down the drive that led away from the main house, passing Mr. Janus along the way. (Mr. Janus had retrieved his own horse, which was quite a sorry nag when compared with the Colonel's steed.)

As soon as the visitors had left, Uncle Robert winked at me and turned to Jeremy. "Jeremy, run out and tell Bartholomew that I want the east field planted before sundown."

I watched with amusement as the slave's eyes nearly bugged out of his head. "But, but, Massa Covington sir, we's still workin' in the *south* field! Dares jus no way. I means... How...?"

"Hmm..... Well there's still two hours of light left. What to do? What to do?" Uncle Robert scratched his head through his dark hair and finally said, "I guess that it will just have to wait. Run out to the south field as fast as you can and tell Bartholomew that he can call it a day. Go and have a nice supper. But I want you to start planting the east field with corn tomorrow. Do you understand?"

"Yas sir, Yas sir, Massa. Tank you! Tank you! With that Jeremy took off at high speed to deliver his message to the slave driver, Bartholomew.

Covey was a great cook, but she was our only house servant, so unfortunately she had many more duties than merely preparing our food. She was the oldest of our slaves, probably about fifty or so. Recently she had asked Mother if her eight-year-old granddaughter Lizzie could help her in the house, and Mother agreed that it was a good idea. Covey had been looking out for Lizzie since Lizzie's mother died two years ago. Lizzie had been a favorite playmate of Ellen and Eliza, but now she was

7

becoming aware of her status. It's strange, but most Negro children do not even know they're slaves until they're eight or nine and finally put to work. I guess it's understandable, since up to that age their time is spent playing right alongside the white children. I guess at first, they think that they're just like us.

After dinner I went looking for Jack. Jack was my dog. He had been my father's and was a good old pooch. Nowadays he usually didn't stray too far from the house, but for some reason I couldn't locate him. I went off behind the house and searched the stable and barn, but I didn't find him in either place. As the sun was beginning to set, I grabbed a lamp from the barn, lit it, and continued down the path toward the "village."

The village was a good half-mile from the house, hidden from view by a grove of maple and pine trees. As I approached the half dozen cabins I could hear "our people" talking and singing. You would think that they would have been all tuckered out after a long day in the fields, but I guess they were excited since Uncle Robert let them knock off early.

As I sauntered into the village I was looking at the small group that was gathered in front of the big oak, about twenty-five yards away, when movement in the shadows made me jump. I was startled as Zeke came around the side of his cabin holding a hoe.

"Oh I's sorry Massa Gid'in. Did I scare ya? I was jus tendin' my plot. Goin' to have some nice carrots befo' too long. Yas sir. What you be doin' out here? You's okay?"

There are many who would have been scared to death of a big buck like Zeke coming at them with a hoe, but I wasn't afraid, just startled. Most planters never allow slaves to take tools back to their cabins with them. They were afraid they'd lose them, hide them so they couldn't work the fields, or even use them to kill whites. Maybe they were right; I mean that business with Nat Turner and all. But, Uncle Robert never thought of things

8

like that. He was pretty lax, and had no problem allowing his people to use his tools to tend to their garden plots.

I recovered quickly as Zeke's wife, Clara, emerged from their cabin carrying their baby, Abram. "No, I'm okay; I'm just looking for Jack. Have you seen him?"

"No, can't say as I have. Clara, you seen Massa Gid'in's dog here 'bouts?"

Clara was gently rocking the infant in her arms. "No, sorry Massa Gid'in I ain't seen that ol' pooch today."

I continued toward the big oak where a half dozen of our people were gathered. Old Cicero was playing the banjo and the others were singing and dancing. I recall reflecting on how happy they were. At the time, I wondered how anyone could think that they would be better off on their own having to fend for themselves in the cruel, real world.

As I came upon the group, Jeremy looked at me fearfully and buried his elbow into the side of Jacob, the slave standing next to him. Apparently, Jacob did not follow this hint. Cicero stopped his playing and looked at me with a wide grin.

"Evenin' Massa Gid'in." Jacob grinned. "I knows you was on da poach with de gentlemens today. Jeremy here was jus tellin' us how he convinced Massa Robert to let us off early. Dat true Massa Gid'in?"

The women began to giggle and the men to roar.

Jeremy quickly broke in. "Massa Gid'in. Dat's not what I said! Dat's not what I said! Massa Robert... he a good man. He knows we couldn't get to dat field today!" With earnest eyes Jeremy finished with: "Massa Gid'in, *please...*"

I did not possess the wit of my uncle or perhaps I would have kept Jeremy on the line by suggesting we ask Bartholomew what message Jeremy had relayed to him.

Bartholomew was not part of the little group by the big oak. He was sitting on a small stool in front his own cabin, whittling. The humor of the moment was lost on me as it merely distracted from my goal of finding Jack. I was about to ask the group if they'd seen my dog, when Bartholomew rose and walked over.

"Alright, you's best be breakin' it up now. You know dat we got a lot of work tomorrow. Bes be gittin' to bed."

Many owners see fit to hire an overseer to manage their slaves, but I've got to tell you, though Bartholomew was only a slave himself, he was as good as any overseer. He knew more about farming than any white man I ever met, and the rest of our people rarely gave him any guff. There's no doubt that they were more afraid of Bartholomew than of Uncle Robert.

The group began to disperse, knowing better than to oppose Bartholomew.

"Wait, wait," I interjected. "Have any of you seen Jack?"

They all responded in the negative.

Bartholomew turned to me. "You bes be gittin' back yoself, Massa Gid'in. It be gittin powerful dark soon. No moon tonight you know. Dat 'ol pooch will show hisself. He probably out after some bitch."

Bartholomew was right, I should be getting back. I hadn't even told Mother or Uncle Robert that I was leaving the house. I ambled back up the path and around the grove of maples and pines, whistling and calling out "Jack!" as I went.

I climbed the broad front steps of the porch, a bit dejected, but less than alarmed. Jack was old, but he still had a little spark left in him. Bartholomew was probably correct; the old hound had picked up the scent of a female. However, as I reached for the doorknob, I was roused when my lamp cast its light on none other than Jack, lying in his familiar spot in the corner. I was delighted to see my old friend and went over to give him a quick scratch on the head when a bit of indignation welled up in me.

"Where were you? Huh? Do you know you made me walk all the way out to the village looking for you?" I chastised the old pooch. He was far from contrite however as he merely yawned in response, dropped his head down onto his forepaw, and went to sleep.

As I put out the lamp and entered the house, I could hear Mother and Uncle Robert talking in the parlor. Few men, at least few southern men, discussed anything of interest with their wives. That sort of activity was left amongst the men folk, and interaction between the sexes remained superficial. This was not the case in our house, though. My mother was educated and curious. She liked the art of discussion. She never flaunted convention by expressing her opinions in the company of other men (and risk embarrassing my uncle) but at home, in private, she could hold her own in any conversation ranging from politics to the sciences. My uncle was not quite as schooled as Mother, but he was intelligent and literate, and the aloofness that was so often irksome to others, allowed Mother to exercise her intellect in our home.

I poked my head into the parlor in time to hear Mother castigating Faust's machinations, her finger indicating the passage she was emphasizing in the open text resting in her lap. Always the scoundrel, Uncle Robert was defending the German's dealings with Mephistopheles and the wide grin on his face left much doubt as to the sincerity of his conviction to his argument.

"Hello Gideon, what can we do for you?" my uncle shot in my direction.

"Um, I just wanted to say good night," I sheepishly replied, realizing that they had not missed my presence from the house.

"Right you are then," Uncle Robert replied.

Mother got up from her chair, folding the book closed on her finger to mark her place. "Alright then Gideon, good night," she responded, tenderly giving me a kiss on the cheek though obviously anxious to get back to her assault on Doctor Faustus

I lit a candle and climbed the stairs, heading for my bedroom. As I passed the girls' room, I opened the door slightly,

11

looking in as was my ritual, to make sure all was well. My candle cast enough light for me to make out the two little dark heads poking out of the quilt, each facing opposite directions in the same bed. I gently closed the door and headed to my own room. I should have gone immediately to sleep knowing that I would have a busy day upon the morrow. I would have to study with Mother in the morning and then rush out to the fields to supervise the planting. I was not much of an overseer, (and after all we had Bartholomew) but Mother wanted me to learn how things worked at The Copper Beeches, knowing that it would one day be mine. However, I could not bring myself to sleep right away. I was anxious to get back to the volume of Shakespeare that I kept on my nightstand. I was deeply involved in the adventure of Henry V. I read until exhaustion overcame me, and drifted off to the fantasy of riding off into battle at Agincourt. "And gentlemen in England now a-bed, shall think themselves accursed they were not here, and hold their manhoods cheap whiles any speaks that fought with us upon Saint Crispin's day!" wrung in my ears as I fell under Morpheus's spell, never imagining how little warfare resembled the romantic recounting of The Bard.

I groggily pulled myself from bed as the roosters announced the break of day. The sky was still pink as the sunlight shoved its way through the sycamore branches that spread themselves in front of my window. The candle on my nightstand had not burned very low; apparently Covey had snuffed it not long after I fell asleep. She had warned me a hundred times not to leave a candle burning while I slept, always chastising me that I would burn the house down. I'll bet she never got to sleep herself until she was sure my light had been extinguished.

I crept past the girls' room and down the stairs for a fine breakfast with Uncle Robert and Mother. Covey's bacon, eggs, and grits satisfied the hunger I had built up riding into battle with King Henry.

I avoided Covey's eyes as she served us, as a precaution against her giving it to me over the candle. Mother would not have appreciated me falling asleep with a candle left burning, so the less she knew about it the better. Covey was protective of me though, so I guess I should have known she would not bring it up in front of Mother, though I was sure to hear about it later in private.

"I have some business to attend to in Fincastle," my uncle said to me, "so I'll need you to get them going on the south field. After you're sure they're on top of things, come back to the house to study with your mother and then get back out there again."

I nodded in affirmation as I dug into my grits.

"Robert," mother broke in politely, "see if Mr. Drower has any writing paper and ink. I am running a bit low."

Mr. Drower ran the local store in Fincastle. He not only sold goods, but was the local commodities trader as well. He acted as an agent for most of the farmers in the immediate area, getting our crops to market. He was also the middleman between the local planters and the miller, Mr. McDonald. Drower was a German immigrant who had set up shop in Fincastle a decade earlier. He was an honest, though humorless man. This lack of wit contrasted greatly with Uncle Robert's demeanor, and my uncle could not resist riling the shopkeeper at every possible opportunity. The German did not appreciate this, and came to dread even the most superficial contact between them. Had I liked him more, I would have advised the merchant to simply laugh along with Uncle Robert a few times, which would have probably caused my uncle to lose interest in jibing him.

After finishing breakfast, I left through the front door, stopping to give old Jack a pat, and then went out to the stables. I saddled and mounted my pony, Ajax, and rode out to the south field. By this time the sun had been up for an hour, and the field hands had already brought the mules and supplies out to the field. The week before, the field had been plowed and since shovel plows like ours left a very light furrow, we could begin to plant. Poor Mr. Janus had an old moldboard plow which left large chunks of earth. He then needed to harrow the field to break up these chunks, and then roll it flat with one of his homemade log rollers. I wonder if our slaves knew how grateful they should be that Father had invested in the right equipment.

As I arrived on the scene, Bartholomew already had things well in hand. He had divided the workers into two gangs. The first group was widening the plow furrows with hoes. Each of the five men in the group was responsible for a row. Following each man was a woman who deposited four or five seeds and then covered the hole with her heel. Our people were exceptionally efficient, and planted the corn without much thought. They sang as they went, the whole of them, (excluding Bartholomew) participating in the call and response of the song.

"Oh, Oh, he's my savior!"
"Oh, Oh who's your savior?"
"Oh, Oh, he's my savior!"
"Oh, Oh, who's your savior?"
"Oh, Oh, he's my savior now!"

The whole field would be planted in this tedious, though efficient manner. There was really little for me to supervise. So, I tied Ajax to a cottonwood and from my jacket pocket removed my Shakespeare. I reclined beneath the tree and dove back into the bard's prose.

It was getting close to noon when I was stirred from my reading by the rattle of pots and pans as the women began preparing lunch for the workers. They began boiling corn meal and cooking bacon, and the aroma reminded me that I should head for home for my own mid-day meal and a bit of study with Mother.

14

"I'll be back in a bit!" I yelled to Bartholomew as I stowed my volume and mounted Ajax. I felt quite foolish saying this, since I was about as needed as a hat on a pig.

"We be right here!" Bartholomew returned with a wave.

Covey served us a delicious stew for lunch, after which the girls and I joined Mother in the parlor for a bit of study. The girls were working in their primers, concentrating on basic reading and writing, while Mother had me performing arithmetic. Mother was not terribly schooled in mathematics, and I had in fact long surpassed her abilities. So, I worked from texts and then checked my own work. I enjoyed arithmetic more than many of the other subjects I studied. I particularly liked its deductive nature. I especially fond of solving algebraic equations and geometric proofs.

I worked on my studies for about two hours, and then headed back out to the fields since Uncle Robert had not yet returned. As was the custom, the slaves were allowed a siesta at lunch that lasted a little over an hour, so upon my return, they were just getting back to work.

Clara and Harriet were cleaning up after the meal, and Clara's baby was sitting in a basket under the cottonwood. Harriet had her husband, Jacob, bring up a wagon so that they could take the pots and utensils back to the village. I waited to dismount until Clara had removed the basket holding little Abram, and placed him in the wagon. She climbed aboard and Jacob drove them back to the village as Harriet went back to work in the field. I climbed down and allowed Ajax to graze in the tall grass behind the cottonwood as I strode out to speak with Bartholomew.

"Afernoon Massa Gid'in," Bartholomew said taking off his hat, though not diverting his eyes from his gangs as he directed them in resuming the job.

"How is everything going?" I asked, feigning an air of authority.

"Jus fine, Jus fine," he replied, interrupting with a shout to Jeremy to hurry up and re-harness the mules who had been allowed to graze during the siesta.

I really didn't like playing overseer, but I had been given a job, and Uncle Robert would want a report when he returned.

"What do you suppose we should do next after this field is planted?" I asked, remembering that Mother wanted me to learn all I could about farming.

"I do believes we should continue in yonder field," he pointed ahead, "and plant de potatoes."

"What about the tobacco?"

"Well, sir, dat a good idea, de seedlings is 'bout ready. But we planted 'baccy in dat field las year an we really got to change de fields. 'Baccy use up de soil somethin' fierce. I tinks we plant de potatoes in yonder field, but we ought lets de seedlings grow another couple weeks in de seed beds, den we plant de 'baccy over in yonder field," he motioned with his pipe to the field behind the cottonwood, "we had rye in dare las season. I tinks de 'baccy will do jus fine over dare."

That Bartholomew sure knew his farming. I remember that I was struck by the fact that Negroes were supposed to be so stupid, but Bartholomew knew more about farming than most men I've met. *He* was teaching *me*.

I stayed out in the south field for the duration of the day, intermittently reading from my book, and observing the slaves at work. Occasionally I would close my eyes and listen to their singing. They are such a rhythmic people. As the sun began to sink low, Bartholomew approached me with his hat in his hands.

"We's all done here, sir. I tinks we should get tings stowed away, and get de supplies and such back to de barns."

"Yes, that sounds like a good idea," I said, again faking an air of leadership. "Get it all taken care of Bartholomew, I'm going to see if Master Robert has returned yet."

16

With that I mounted my horse and trotted off toward the house. I could hear Bartholomew barking orders as I rode away. Given Uncle Robert's demeanor, and my lack of experience, we sure were lucky to have a driver like Bartholomew. I wondered how much he was worth. Surly he could fetch more than any other slave in the county. As I rode, I speculated how much he could have earned as an overseer if he were free.

I took Ajax to the stable, unsaddled and stalled him, and threw in some hay for him to munch. As I walked up to the house, I could see Uncle Robert approaching up the drive. Astonishingly he was not alone. Seated in the rear of the buckboard was a black form completely unfamiliar to me. Surprises were not abundant in this sleepy part of Virginia and just who this fellow might be was intriguing to say the least.

17

CHAPTER 2

"Gideon! Fetch Jeremy or Zeke!" Uncle Robert shouted, as he brought the wagon to a halt and set the brake. "Hurry now!"

Despite my overwhelming curiosity, I recovered my senses and set off at a run to the barn where the slaves were just getting the wagons housed and mules stabled. I grabbed Jeremy by the arm, and beckoned him to follow.

"Aww. What for, Massa Gid'in? I jus wants to git to my cabin an have some supper. Does I have to, Massa?"

"Enough. Jeremy! Don't make me take the riding crop to you!" I said, looking at the tool hanging from a nearby pole, even though I doubt I had the nerve to use it. "Master Robert wants you in the front of the house immediately."

"Massa Robert's back? I be right dare," he said, changing his tune. "Here, Zeke!" he yelled down the length of the barn. "Take dis here mule, Massa Robert sent young Massa here to fetch me!"

I had already begun my run back to the house by the time Jeremy had handed the reins to Zeke, but he was quickly on my heels.

There was still a bit of light left as we made it to the front of the house. By now Uncle Robert was standing on the front porch talking to Mother. The girls, as well as Covey and Lizzie had joined them, curiously examining the strange buck.

"Ah, Jeremy. Good. This is Ulysses. He is a new addition to our family here at The Copper Beeches. Take the wagon down to the barn and stable the horses, and then introduce Ulysses to everyone in the village. Make sure that Bartholomew meets him. Then set him up with a bunk in your cabin. Make sure he gets some supper too. Tell Bartholomew I'll be out to see him later. Okay, off with you now," he curtly ordered through that sly smile of his.

Jeremy listened intently to Uncle Robert's instructions, but kept stealing glances at the new slave. Ulysses was a big buck, not quite as big as Zeke, though. He was probably five feet ten inches in height, with a well-formed, muscular build. His skin was blacker than night itself. None of our other people were nearly as dark as the new farm hand. The young man stood in silence, smiling broadly. The daylight was fading quickly, and the new slave's teeth fairly glowed as he stood completely erect, with his hands behind his back. All eyes were scrutinizing this curious new slave.

"Yas sir, Massa Robert. Yas sir. Come on now," Jeremy said, apparently to the horses as he turned them toward the barn, "You too, you too, fella, come on now," he continued to Ulysses, snapping his fingers.

Knowing Jeremy, I'm sure he would have beleaguered Uncle Robert with countless questions had he not been eager for supper. As I ascended the steps, I peered around the side of the house as Jeremy led Ulysses down the lane toward the barn. I was about to ask my uncle how he came to acquire the new slave, when he anticipated my question.

"Let's get some supper shall we? I'll fill all of you in during supper. It's a good one, it's a good one..." he chuckled, as he waited for my mother and the girls to lead the way to the table.

Normally we would have already eaten by now, but Mother insisted on waiting for her husband. We sat down at the table and Covey and Lizzie began to serve us the meal that had been kept warm in the kitchen. Uncle Robert remained silent for a while as we all anxiously awaited the story. Even Covey cast curious glances in his direction as she placed portions of the roast on each plate. Finally he said: "I'm really hungry, perhaps I'll save the tale of brave Ulysses until after dinner."

19

Ellen, Eliza, and I all let out a frustrated groan in unison. Covey even let slip "Lordy now!" She quickly apologized however, and shuffled back to the kitchen flush with embarrassment.

Thankfully Mother interjected, "Robert, that's enough. You made no mention of us acquiring more help. There must be a lively reason for coming home with this fellow. Let's have the explanation, please."

Uncle Robert succumbed to the wishes of his spouse. "Well, it's quite a story." Dabbing the corner of his mouth with his napkin, he shook his head in a bemused chuckle. "You remember Tom Owens?"

Mother nodded. "He passed on last year, didn't he?"

"Yes. His place was about twenty miles or so on the other side of Fincastle," he directed toward my cousins and me. "Well, among his people was this buck Ulysses. Ulysses was a strong, reliable fellow and Mr. Owens' eldest son, James, you remember James, he died in the last year of the war with Mexico," he turned again toward my mother. "Anyway, James took Ulysses along to carry a load of grain down river into North Carolina. They boarded the barge themselves to accompany the crop because Owens had some business down there that required his personal attention. Well once the grain had been delivered, James decided to stay in Winston-Salem for a few days. Unfortunately for James, he got himself into a bit of a scrape. It seems that he embroiled himself in a card game where he fell deeply into debt. The only recourse he had to relieve this debt was to hand over poor Ulysses. James knew that his father would be livid if the truth were revealed, so he concocted a fabulous story where Ulysses had fallen into the river and drowned." He took a sip from his glass before continuing, "Well, Ulysses had a wife at the Owens' place and she went hysterical with grief. The very sight of James sent her into fits.

20

As a result, she was worthless to the Owens's. Jacob sold her, quite cheaply, to someone not far from here."

At this, Uncle Robert waited. Chewing his food slowly, he quenching his thirst with a gulp of cider. Mercifully, he continued.

"Her name is Penelope, but she goes by 'Penny.' Perhaps you know her as she is the property of our neighbor Henry Janus."

I did indeed know the girl, though I doubt if Mother did, and certainly the two young ones didn't, as they rarely left The Copper Beeches. Penny was a comely negress, perhaps twenty-three or twenty-four years of age. I had seen here numerous times at the market, and on the Janus farm. She always appeared to be very quiet and shy, a polite and industrious girl; and whether due to her isolation on the Janus farm or from sheer heartbreak, had not taken up with another man.

My musings were interrupted as my uncle continued. "Let me see if I can remember this properly..." He tapped a finger upon his pursed lips. "The man who had won Ulysses, sold him to a trader, who put him up for auction in Kentucky. He was bought by a man named Kruger who kept him for the harvest and then in turn sold him to another trader who relieved himself of Ulysses in Tennessee, selling him to a cotton broker."

Uncle Robert paused for a moment; evidently consulting his memory to ensure that he was recounting the complicated story correctly. Finally he commenced. "Recently, the broker, a man by the name of Hoskins, had business in Richmond, but had to stop in Fincastle to recover payment for some cattle he had had herded through the valley. Since he was aware that Ulysses was familiar with the area, he brought him along. I was leaving Mr. Drower's store when I recognized the slave whose drowning Tom Owens had lamented to me five years earlier. I was quite amazed to see the fellow, and queried him as to how he

21

happened to be living and breathing. He recounted his amazing story to me."

"His story touched a nerve in me," my uncle shrugged a bit sheepishly as he worked his knife through the beef on his plate, "so I went back into Drower's and negotiated his purchase from this Mr. Hoskins. I'll admit, I paid a bit more than he's worth, but he knows Shenandoah farming since he's from the area, and I thought it would be very Christian of me to bring him to The Copper Beeches, not five miles from the Janus farm where his wife now resides."

The story was indeed fantastic. Many slave families were broken up by sale or death, and the victim of the former had about as much chance of finding his way home as the latter. This Ulysses had suffered both, in a manner of speaking, and yet arrived back in Botetourt County, to live in the vicinity of his presumed widowed wife. Uncle Robert's account certainly explained the bright smile that had been pasted on the buck's face.

Mother was awash with commendation for Uncle Robert's forethought and generosity, praising his Christian ethics and compassion. My uncle continued to eat his meal through Mother's flattering, flashing me a wink between bites. Mother was not the only one impressed by the act. For the remainder of the meal Covey's face beamed. Although she had been in the kitchen during the tale, her countenance demonstrated that her hearing had lost none of its acuity despite her age.

The next day was Saturday, which meant a half-day of work, and of course there would be no work on the Sabbath. Some of our people were given passes to town on Saturday afternoon or Sunday after service to sell the products of their garden plots in the market square. Others preferred to stay close to home, spending time in the village with their families. This being the case, I knew that there would be opportunity for Ulysses to travel

22

to Janus' place, *if Uncle Robert allowed it*. After all, he was new to us and his security could not be guaranteed. It would not do for our newest slave to take off after a half-day at The Copper Beeches. Uncle Robert however answered the question I had been silently pondering.

"After work tomorrow, I'll take Ulysses over to Deep Dene."

Deep Dene was the name of the small ravine that ran through the Janus place, and Mr. Janus had assumed the name for his farm in hopes that it would make his property sound more akin to the plantations of the gentry.

"I expect that he will cause quite a stir!" my Uncle smiled, obviously thinking of the shock Penny would experience at the revelation of her husband's survival. "Well, old Henry shouldn't mind Ulysses making weekend trips to his place," he considered. "He always gives the girl off on Sundays anyway."

"Can I go with you?" I asked.

"Sure, I reckon so."

I usually jumped at any chance to travel beyond The Copper Beeches, but I have to admit, I was also anxious to see the reunion of Ulysses and his wife. I envisioned it as being quite a heartwarming spectacle.

After dinner, I decided to accompany Uncle Robert out to the village to see that Jeremy had followed his instructions. We stepped out onto the front porch, and as Uncle Robert lit a lamp I gave old Jack a scratch on the head.

"Come on now, Gideon. You're coming aren't you?" Uncle Robert chided mischievously as he started off. I hurried after him, leaving Jack to his favorite spot.

"How did we make out today?" my uncle asked, as we trod down the path.

"The corn is all planted, and Bartholomew thinks we should start potatoes in the next field.

"What do you think of that idea?" my uncle prodded me, his smirk illuminated by the lamp's glow.

"I think it's a fine idea. We planted wheat there last year and potatoes always seem to grow well in an old grain field."

"You've been listening to Bartholomew! Wonderful, wonderful! Your mother will be quite proud." He tussled my hair as he finished: "We'll make a planter out of you yet, Mr. Book Learning."

The sky was cloudy, but that mattered little since it was still a new moon. We had to walk slowly as the lantern's light seemed to be swallowed up by the night. Eventually we rounded the grove of maples and pines, and the village came into view. The cabins themselves couldn't be seen but the light from inside seeped between the cracks of the cabin walls.

Our first stop was at Bartholomew's cabin. Uncle Robert rapped on the door, calling out: "Bartholomew, its me." as he stepped inside. Most masters would not even consider knocking on a slave's door, but my uncle always did so before he entered.

"Hallo, Massa Robert!" Bartholomew greeted, placing the pipe on the table that had rested between his teeth.

"Do you mind if we sit down?" For some reason Uncle Robert was always courteous to his slaves.

"Yas, sir, has yoself a seat," the driver replied, motioning to the crude table.

"Thank you."

"Can I gets you gentlemans some coffee?" Bartholomew asked, going for the pot boiling in the fireplace.

"No, no. We won't be staying long. Please, sit down with us. Did you meet Ulysses?"

"Yas sir. He looks to be a fine buck. I sure is glad you was able to get another hand befo' the plantin' is done. I drives de gangs mighty hard, but dares only so much dey can do. I thinks you made a fine idea gettin' another hand."

"Did he get fixed up in Jeremy's cabin like I said?"

"Yas sir but we didn't have any extra bunks, so we jus threw some hay in de corner. Maybe tomorrow we can build him a

24

proper bunk." Bartholomew scratched at his chin. "If you don't mind me askin' Massa, what be wit dat fella?"

"How do you mean?" my uncle threw him a quizzical look.

"Well sir, he be smilin' from ear to ear, but ain't nobody can figure out why."

My uncle smirked, and laughed silently to himself. "Did you ask him?"

"Well, sir wit dat grin, I thought he was sassin' me, so I raised my hand to give him a smack, but Jeremy told me he was a grinnin' since you brung him in. I figures he ain't sassin' me, so I asks him, but he jus say 'he happy,' and asks fo some food. So I has him eat wit Jeremy and I gets mysef some vittles. I was jus finishin' my own supper when you and Massa Gid'in came in."

My uncle rose, stating, "Well, I'm going to go down to Jeremy's cabin and make sure our new fellow is okay." With a wink and a pat on my back he said, "Gideon, you fill Bartholomew here in on why Ulysses is smiling."

With that, Uncle Robert grabbed the lantern and let himself out of the cabin. Bartholomew returned the pipe to his mouth and peered at me with a very determined look, as if he wanted to be sure to comprehend every word I said. I recounted my uncle's dinner story as best I could. Bartholomew let me complete the story in full before relenting his dogged gaze. After I had finished, he leaned back in his chair and removed the pipe from his mouth to sound a low whistle.

"Dat's some story. I suppose he be itchin' to see his wife," Bartholomew pondered, taking a couple of puffs on his pipe.

"Uncle Robert plans to take him over to Deep Dene tomorrow, after you get some work done."

"Massa Robert was always good 'bout lettin' me see my wife... He a good man."

Bartholomew peered expressionlessly into the fire and continued to puff away on his pipe. He vacantly stared into the

25

flames, and for a good half-minute we sat in silence. I surmised that Bartholomew was thinking about his own family. Bartholomew had had a wife over at Chiltern Grange. They had been married a few years when she learned she was with child. Unfortunately, she died giving birth, and the child, a boy, died a few days later. It occurred to me at that moment that perhaps Bartholomew's vigor as a driver was some sort of a way to take his mind off of his loss. I had heard of cases where people try to throw themselves into an activity to distract them from their woes.

I figured that I would leave Bartholomew to his introspections, and awkwardly bid my farewell. "I think I'll go down to Jeremy's and see how things are." I don't think Bartholomew heard this, but as I rose, the scrape of the chair roused him.

"Okay den. Okay den. I sees you later Massa Gid'in," he said, rising respectfully.

I briskly left the cabin and headed toward that of Jeremy. As I got half way there, Uncle Robert emerged from the hut and strode toward me bearing the lantern.

"How is everything?" I asked, wishing I'd made it to the cabin before he emerged. I was curious to see for myself how our new hand was doing.

"He's asleep already! Can you beat that? I guess he was on the road all day, and it tuckered him out," my uncle stated. "I didn't even get to tell him that we'd go over to Deep Dene tomorrow. Oh well, let's get home. Even though tomorrow is Saturday, we've a lot to do."

As we walked back up the path past the grove of maples and pines, I recall musing over the exhaustion of the new slave. He must have been either completely wiped out, or a very cool fellow. He *must* be excited about seeing his wife. I remember thinking that *I* could never sleep when I was excited. Before I knew it we were back at the house. I bid my uncle and mother

26

good night, and retired. I peaked in on the girls, and settled into bed with Shakespeare, but I couldn't seem to stay focused. I kept thinking about Ulysses. His travels, his miraculous return, and the elation he and his wife would feel seeing one another again. I eventually gave up on reading, extinguished the candle (wouldn't Covey be proud!) and tried to sleep. Unfortunately my mind kept wandering back to Ulysses. I don't know what hour it was by the time I finally drifted off.

After breakfast I accompanied Uncle Robert on his weekly inspection of the plantation. We traveled out to the barn where we checked the horses and the adjoining pen where the cattle were housed. There we saddled our own horses since the slaves were all out in the fields. Next we rode around to the hog pen, and as we expected, Zeke and Cicero had already fed them. From there we proceeded past the chicken house where the hens had also already been attended. We trotted off northeast of the house to where our other outbuildings lie. A gentle breeze was blowing in from that direction, so I could smell the wonderful scent of the cured pork from the smokehouse. Behind the smokehouse was the bee house whose inhabitants were already leaving their hives in search of pollen. We rode by the springhouse as well, its curious stone structure peeking out of the ground. We were fortunate; we had a vivacious, fresh spring in ours, which kept our dairy goods nicely chilled.

Most who knew me at the time were fully aware that I'd rather have had my nose in a book than attend to the duties of a planter, but I actually enjoyed these rides around the plantation. The Copper Beeches was the only home I'd ever known, and I felt connected to it. The outbuildings, granary, animals, even the village, all seemed a part of me. Surely I dreamed of Richmond, the sea, England, and all of the places I visited in my readings, but deep down part of me never really wanted to leave my home in the Valley of Virginia.

After we had completed our inspection, we prepared to head out to see how the slaves were progressing. "I wonder if Ajax is fast enough to beat old Ruston here?" Uncle Robert commented, patting his horse.

I was about to take the bait when he continued, "My heavens, what's that? Is the house on fire?"

Alarmed, I turned one hundred eighty degrees to look back at the house when I heard Uncle Robert yell "Ya!" and spur his horse toward the fields, laughing as he galloped off. I should have expected as much. I was a tolerable rider at best, so my uncle hardly needed such deception to beat me in a race, but he could not resist. Recovering my composure, I hurried after him at a less than frantic gait.

By the time I arrived out at the field, Uncle Robert had already dismounted, and was speaking with Bartholomew. The field hands were hard at work planting potatoes. They were following much the same procedure as with the corn. One worker widened the plowed furrow with his hoe, a second deposited the seed potato, and a third closed the hole. Our people were making good progress. As I rode up, I scanned the hands for Ulysses. He was planting a row with Jeremy and Jacob, and was working diligently. He fit right in. It looked as if he'd been working our land for years. I dismounted and led my horse over to where Uncle Robert and Bartholomew were standing.

"Oh, Gideon! Glad you could make it," Uncle Robert jibed with a wink, and then returned to his conversation with his driver.

"So, how are things going out here? What is it? Potatoes today?" he asked Bartholomew.

"Yas sir. Potatoes. We doin' jus fine. By Monday I 'spect we have dis field all done. Dees seed potatoes is pretty good. Dat's not always true you know. I tinks we goin' to get a good crop out dees here potatoes."

28

"What about the tobacco?" my uncle queried, running his fingers through his dark hair.

"Well sir, I tinks we give dose seedlings another two weeks, den dey be ready to move out to de fields. I checked on dem dis mornin' and dey's lookin' good."

"Very well, very well." my uncle replied, nodding. "How is the wheat looking?"

"It lookin' good. In a couple of months it be ready to harvest."

We grew a lot of different crops, but our main cash crop was wheat. We sold our tobacco, but we could never compete with the eastern planters, so wheat had evolved as the major cash crop from the Shenandoah Valley.

"How is our new fellow doing?" my uncle asked, waving his hat toward Ulysses.

"He looks to be a hard worker. I tinks you made yoself a good buy on dat dare boy."

"Very good. Keep them at it until noontime, and then pack it in. Tell Ulysses to clean himself up after work and then come up to the house. After lunch Gideon and I will take him over to Deep Dene."

We often took our mid-day meal in the kitchen rather than in the dining room, and we had just finished when there was a soft knock on the kitchen door, which was also the slaves' entrance. Covey opened it to find Ulysses standing with his hat in his hands smiling into the room.

"Dat new boy out here Massa," Covey informed my uncle.

"Show him in, show him in." Uncle Robert replied wiping his mouth with his napkin.

Upon catching sight of Ulysses, Uncle Robert expressed disappointment. "This will never do. Yes, Ulysses, I'm glad that you washed as I had instructed, but those clothes! Oh, those

29

clothes! You've been toiling out in fields all day in those clothes!"

The smile quickly departed the slave's face. "I knows it Massa. But everyting I owns is back wit my ol' massa. Dis is all I's got."

"I suppose that's true..." Uncle Robert scratched his dark head. "Lizzie, come here." Covey's granddaughter quickly put down the dish she was washing and rushed over to us.

"Yes, Massa?" the cute little colored girl asked.

"Lizzie, go into the walnut wardrobe in my bed chamber and bring me the suit of clothes hanging all the way to the right. Do you know where I mean?"

"Yes, Massa."

"You're sure? Which hand is your right hand?" he queried the little girl.

"Dis here," she replied, lifting the correct appendage.

"Okay," he smiled. "Off with you then."

"Now Ulysses," my uncle said turning once again to the field hand, "I am going to give you an old suit of mine. It is old mind you, but it is much better than those clothes you're wearing. I will get you an extra set of work clothes on Monday, and you can use this old suit of mine as your Sunday clothes for now. I am sure that your wife will sew you some nice Sunday clothes once she sees you're not dead." Uncle Robert flashed Mother a smile, who had been sitting quietly at the table admiring the whole exchange.

"Tank you Massa. I's mighty grateful," Ulysses said quietly, diverting his eyes to the floor, though the broad smile had returned to his face.

The patter of little feet could be heard coming down the back stairs. "Ah here's Lizzie." Taking the suit from her, Uncle Robert held it up against Ulysses. "Yes, I think these will fit. Go put these on and then tell Jeremy to rig up the buckboard. Gideon and I will be out directly." With that Ulysses quietly

30

backed his way out of the kitchen and was off running toward the barn.

"Robert, what a kind thought. He really should look his best at this reunion. Just make sure you leave that suit with him. I don't want you wearing it again," Mother stated.

"No, of course not!" laughed Uncle Robert.

In a few minutes we went out to the barn and were met by Jeremy, Bartholomew and Ulysses.

"De buckboard all rigged, Massa." Jeremy said smiling.

"Massa, you sure you don't want de buggy? I can have Jeremy here drive you." Bartholomew asked.

Jeremy flashed Bartholomew an unappetizing look at this suggestion, as he didn't want any chore to cut into his free time.

"No, no. We're taking Ulysses here with us remember? We'll need the buckboard."

"Um, Massa..." Bartholomew said, "Is it okay if a few of de people goes to de market? Some of dem has vegetables dey wants to sell."

"Yes, certainly." Uncle Robert replied, climbing aboard the wagon and grabbing the reins.

"But Massa," Bartholomew hurried, fearing my uncle about to take off, "Massa dey needs a pass."

"Of course." Uncle Robert smiled at his forgetfulness. "Gideon run to the house and fetch me a pass, ink and pen."

I ran to the study and quickly secured the desired objects and returned directly. Ulysses was already sitting anxiously in the rear of the buckboard. My uncle took the implements and listed the slaves Bartholomew said wanted to head to the market. *Zeke, Clara, Abram, Jacob, and Harriet* were scribbled on the pass, which he then handed to Bartholomew. "Here," he said, handing the overseer the pen and ink. "Have Lizzie return that to my study."

31

"You know," Uncle Robert said to me as I climbed aboard, "I think maybe we'll go to the market instead. That might be a good idea."

I could almost feel the wagon shudder as the slave's heart broke.

"Come on now!" I remonstrated my uncle. I saw his witticism as cruel. Many of our slaves had known him all of their lives and yet were too daft to recognize his humor, a new addition like Ulysses had no hope of deciphering his wit.

"All right, it's off to Deep Dene then. Heya!" he nudged the horses forward and off we went.

The Janus property was just a few miles away. Henry Janus was a man about forty. He was of Scotch-Irish stock, a rough looking, burly man used to a hard life. His wife was of the same cast, a hearty woman who was often seen working in the fields with her husband and their three slaves. The Janus's had no children, which was unusual. The rumor was that the deficiency was with Mr. Janus. The evidence of this is somewhat dubious. Some whispered that as a teenager, prior to her courtship with Mr. Janus, Mrs. Janus had miscarried a child whose father remains unknown. Whether this is true is completely speculative, but nonetheless, the Janus's were forced to remain dependent upon their slaves for their labor source as they had no offspring to share in their labors.

As we approached the Janus land, we turned off the road and down the dirt drive that led to the house. About half way up the lane we crossed the wooden bridge that allowed passage over a narrow section of the Deep Dene. The creek that flowed beneath passed through a dam before emptying into a small pond on the Janus farm. At the far end of the pond, the water gurgled through a second dam before continuing through the dene. Mr. Janus had constructed the pond for irrigation purposes, but also to provide himself a place to fish. He loved fishing, and would often be found in his rowboat stalking the pond's catfish and bass.

The Janus house was a log cabin, crude in comparison to our house, but fairly standard for the farmers of the valley. Most owners preferred to keep the slave quarters out of sight of their homes, but the slave cabins were only a short distance from the house. They were two poorly built shacks, one for the two male slaves (Gus and his son Cy) and one for Ulysses' wife Penny. It was probably to the Janus's advantage that the slaves were so close since they all lived and worked together. Also, the proximity of the slave cabins made the Janus home look more appealing when juxtaposed with the ungainly slave quarters.

As we approached the dwellings I could see that all were at the same chore, though in different places. The Janus's and their slaves were all working independent garden plots behind their respective abodes.

Uncle Robert halted the team and set the brake. Mr. Janus straightened his stiff back and shaded his eyes with his hand as he tried to identify his visitors. Uncle Robert removed the mystery by calling out a hearty "Hello!"

"Is that you, Mr. Covington?" Mr. Janus responded. Letting his hoe drop, he ambled over leaving his wife to continue working in the garden.

"Hello, Henry." Uncle Robert greeted, shaking the farmer's dirty hand.

"What brings you out here?" Janus responded, smiling. It wasn't often that he had visitors, and he was obviously honored by the event.

"Henry, this boy here; come here Ulysses..." the slave sprung off the rear of the wagon and came over, "Well... remember when you bought Penny from old Tom Owens? Remember he sold her because she went crazy because her husband had died on that trip with James? Well it turns out her husband didn't really die. This is her husband!"

33

At this revelation, the smile fled Mr. Janus's face. He looked at Ulysses with a confused, pitiful expression. It was quite inexplicable. I didn't expect him to be overjoyed, but I thought he might be somewhat pleased that one of his people would be made happy. My uncle didn't seem to notice Janus's change in demeanor and roused him from this state as he continued.

"I'm sure you won't mind calling Penny to come meet her husband." Uncle Robert beamed at the possibility.

Instead, Mr. Janus turned back to Ulysses, who himself was beaming. "Yonder is her cabin," he said in a surly tone as he pointed to the crude hut, "She's out back tending her plot. Go ahead around."

Ulysses looked at my uncle, who nodded his assent, and the buck was off quick as a flash. I was quite disappointed. I had made the trip to see the reunion; however I had to content myself with the negress's loud cry of joy that emanated from behind the cabin.

Later, on the ride home Uncle Robert said he didn't mind missing the reunion since he felt that relations between a husband and wife should really remain private. This however, did little to sooth my disappointment. At that moment I tried to imagine the scene in my mind's eye: Penny, at work in her garden, with her back to her approaching husband. A strangely familiar voice calls her name. Quivering, she drops her hoe, almost afraid to turn around. She forces herself to look, rubs her eyes to see if she's dreaming, then lets out the cry of elation. The couple run to each other and embrace, hugging and kissing one another. Penny, overcome with joy, begs her lover to explain the miracle of his reappearance. Whether this is what really occurred I would never know; but it is the picture that I painted at the time.

I was shaken back to reality as Mr. Janus asked us if we'd like some coffee, and we accompanied him up to the house. He

34

yelled for his wife to bring the beverages as we took seats at the small pine table on the rustic front porch. In a matter of minutes Mrs. Janus appeared with a pot and cups, served us, and then went back to her gardening. Ulysses was new to us, so Uncle Robert didn't trust him enough to issue him a pass and let him walk home on his own, so he deliberately tarried to give the couple some time to reunite. Once Ulysses had demonstrated himself trustworthy, Uncle Robert would allow him to make the trip on his own.

Uncle Robert regaled Mr. Janus with the story of Ulysses' resurrection and return, but the farmer did not seem impressed. I was quite surprised. Illiterate men like Mr. Janus couldn't get stories from books, so they usually were ardent listeners if someone saw fit to tell them one. However, Janus seemed in a fog. He was only quasi-attentive, and not the jocular host he had proved to be on the half-dozen other occasions I had accompanied my uncle to Deep Dene.

After about an hour we were ready to leave. Mr. Janus could not really be called inhospitable, but his lethargy certainly did not entice us to prolong our visit. Uncle Robert leaned back in his chair and gazed toward Penny's cabin. He removed his pocket-watch and tapped his forefinger on his lips.

"Henry, will you be attending services tomorrow?" my uncle queried Mr. Janus.

"Huh? Oh, yes. Yes, of course." the distracted man replied.

"Well do you suppose you can make sure that Ulysses accompanies Penny? We can retrieve him after the service. We must be going and I'd hate to interrupt the happy couple..." He smirked as he cast another look at the occupied cabin.

"I reckon so," Janus replied, gazing down and gently, yet repeatedly, kicking the leg of the table.

"All right then. Thank you for your hospitality, Henry." Uncle Robert gave him a hearty handshake, and in a minute we were back aboard the wagon retracing our path home.

"He didn't seem too happy, did he?" I asked my uncle.

"Well, he's a yeoman. You never know how many problems farmers like him are suffering through. We're lucky we've got enough slaves, and good land. Janus there has that mucky creek running through his farm and all that uneven ground. You just never know how many problems the other fellow has."

My uncle's analysis made sense. Men of the valley are hearty, and don't burden others with their troubles. We were always taught that to be a man meant shouldering the load yourself. However, I couldn't help recalling Mr. Janus's gregarious greeting. His change in demeanor was subtle, but not unobservable; at least not to me. I thought it odd but did not give it much more thought as my uncle began to needle me about the "race" he'd won earlier in the day.

The next morning we prepared for church. We all dressed in our Sunday best and met in the kitchen for a hearty breakfast. After we ate, Covey and Lizzie put on their Sunday clothes and joined the other colored folk as they made their way past the house. They had all dressed their best, and had to set out early, as they had to walk to Fincastle for services. Zeke had made sure that our coach was rigged up, as Jeremy normally drove us into Fincastle for service. We cleaned up after breakfast and waited on the front porch for Jeremy to bring the coach around. After ten minutes, Uncle Robert grew impatient and walked out to the barn. He returned a few minutes later, driving the team himself.

"That damned Jeremy..." he muttered. "Playing sick again, I recon."

"Robert! It's Sunday after all!" Mother scolded his profanity.

"You're right, you're right," Uncle Robert replied, the smile returning to his face. "I'll deal with him when I get home. Everyone aboard!"

36

He set the brake and dismounted, helping the girls and mother into the carriage. In a matter of minutes we were off to Fincastle.

Both our family and our slaves attended the Baptist Church in town. Of course the colored folk sat in the balcony, but still we worshipped together. Our congregation was made up mainly of the few planters of English stock like ourselves and the Jeffers, and the area's more prosperous yeoman farmers and merchants. Of course Mr. Drower, and others of German descent attended the Trinity Lutheran Church founded by the "Dunkards."

The Dunkards were an odd bunch. They were Germans who had settled in Germantown, Pennsylvania, but many had migrated to the southern part of our valley. They were clannish and sought neither wealth nor prestige. Drower was not a Dunkard per se but I suspect he liked the opportunity to associate with his kinsman.

The valley residents of Scotch-Irish stock, like Mr. Janus, attended Fincastle's Presbyterian church. Though they generally had less slaves (if any) than the members of our congregation, they also reserved their balcony for their people.

As we entered town and passed the Presbyterian congregation, we caught sight of Ulysses walking arm-in-arm with Penny. Uncle Robert drew the team to a halt alongside the couple.

"Hello there Ulysses. How are you getting along?" my uncle bellowed from the driver's seat.

"Jus fine," he bashfully returned, smiling.

"Would you like to accompany Penny to the Presbyterian service?" my uncle asked.

"Yas sir, if it alright."

"Sure, just meet us right here after the service. Do you understand?"

"Yas sir I be right here."

37

As we drove on, Mother confronted my uncle. "Robert, don't you think all of our people should attend our church? Not only does it look bad-- But they're Presbyterians!"

"Aw Elizabeth, let him be with his wife. It doesn't really matter if they come with us or not, as long as they get Jesus. How far above the darkies do you think those Presbyterians are anyway?" he laughed heartily at his joke.

"Oh, I suppose. Perhaps we can get both of them to start attending our services in the future."

"Maybe, maybe." Uncle Robert mused, scratching his head.

As I sat through the service, I tried to stay focused on Reverend Duckenfield's words, but my mind kept wandering. The planting, Ulysses, Mr. Janus, and of course my recent companion, Shakespeare, whose stories unfortunately interested me more than those of the man at the pulpit. I knew that there is no more important time to be attentive than at church, but my mind just wouldn't cooperate.

CHAPTER 3

After church we mingled in town for a while. After all, Sunday was the only time we regularly saw our neighbors. Our service had ended before that of the Presbyterians, and we had to wait for Ulysses anyway. It was a nice bright day, and a pleasant breeze carried the scent of pine needles from the wood beyond the churchyard. The adults socialized around the front of the church as the children ran about playing tag. One group of boys was having a contest to see how far they could throw rocks. I, as usual, congregated with the adults listening intently to their conversations. I was trying to focus on that of my uncle, Colonel Jeffers, and Mr. Mason, who had renewed the discussion on the proposed Compromise of 1850, when my mother shooed me away, insisting that I join the other children. I always thought it odd that she only insisted that I interact with the other children when at such functions. At The Copper Beeches she never pushed me to go out and frolic. In fact she encouraged my bookish behavior. I suppose perhaps she was concerned that I appear the same as the other children when in public.

Reluctantly I ambled over to the group of boys throwing the rocks. There was Johnny McPherson, Henry Hillston, George O'Shea, Bucky Steed and a few other boys whom I can't really recall. Awkwardly, I tried to fit in. Though invited, I really had no desire to join the contest. I was not a weak boy, but most of the others were bigger than I, and much more practiced in the raucous skill of rock throwing. I did however offer some advice. I explained to Henry that though his arm was undeniably stronger than that of his chief competitor (George), the parabola of his arc was too shallow, and therefore unless he adjusted his aim, he would never outdistance him in his throw. Henry was a rough-and-tumble kind of a fellow and looked at me as though I had three heads. He did not heed my advice, (if he even understood it) and needless to say his toss fell short. This incident turned out to be rather ironic as Henry was later to serve in the Botetourt Virginia Artillery. I wonder if my advice on his trajectory ever influenced his gun placement? Perhaps he recalled that rock-throwing contest a decade earlier.

After about an hour we prepared to head home. Many were staying to picnic on the church grounds given it was such a nice day, and we had often lingered to participate in such events ourselves but Mother wanted to return to The Copper Beeches. She said that we should spend some time together at home, which I knew to mean that she was reading a book that happened to be more entertaining than her present company.

The Presbyterian service had since let out, and it's congregates were employed in a similar activity as ourselves. As we loaded into our carriage I could see Ulysses and Penny waiting exactly where my uncle had instructed, though I didn't recall him saying that *Penny* should wait there as well. The other colored folk had assembled under a tall pine at the end of the street, preparing to walk back to their respective homes. We drove out of town and pulled up alongside Ulysses and his wife.

"Are you ready to go back home now, Ulysses?" Uncle Robert asked.

"Yas Massa. Massa…" Ulysses bashfully pawed at the ground with his foot. "Does you tink Penelope can come back wit me? I means jus fo de res of de day…"

"Hmm. Well…you see Ulysses the problem is that if she were to visit, she would eventually have to head home and I don't think Penny should travel back to Deep Dene alone, and unfortunately you haven't been with us long enough that I can trust you to take her. Besides, I'm not sure Mr. Janus would approve." My uncle scratched at his chin. "No. No, I don't think so. As soon as you prove yourself to be hard working and

40

trustworthy, I'll give you weekend passes to Deep Dene. But today, I think you'll have to come home yourself."

Ulysses quietly responded "Okay, Massa. I understand. I goin' to show you. I be de bes worker on de plantation."

"You say your goodbyes and then walk back home with the rest of our people. Penny where's Mr. Janus?"

"He be inside talkin' wit de pastor, sir," the negress meekly replied.

A familiar smirk began to creep across my uncle's face.

"You know, I am in an unusually happy mood today. I suspect that it may have been Reverend Duckenfield's moving sermon. I have changed my mind. Penelope you may come back to The Copper Beeches if Mr. Janus says it's alright. I'll have one of the other hands ride you home."

Ulysses was overjoyed. "Tank you, Massa!" he praised my uncle before sending Penny off to implore her master.

Before riding out of town, Uncle Robert halted the team by the large pine and instructed Bartholomew to make sure that Ulysses accompanied our people home and Penny too, if Mr. Janus consented.

"By the way Bartholomew, what happened to Jeremy? As you can see, I'm driving the team myself."

"He didn't talk to you?" Bartholomew asked, the anger apparent on his face. "He said he was sick. He said he was goin' to ask you if'n he could stay at de Copper Beeches today." I's goin' to tear him up when I gets back!"

"No, do nothing of the kind. I'll speak to you about it later. Don't worry yourself." With that Uncle Robert smacked the horse with his crop and off we went.

Sunday was always observed as the day of rest, and as I already related, at times we stayed in Fincastle congregating at church. Other times we visited our neighbors, or they visited us. Still there were instances like this particular Sunday, that we returned home to spend time together as a family. This day was a bit unique however.

After we reached The Copper Beeches, Uncle Robert left Mother and the girls off at the house, and then we proceeded to take the carriage to the barn. We hitched the team to the post, knowing the Zeke would attend to the coach and horses when he got back. We then returned to the house to find the girls and Mother in the kitchen preparing food and placing it in large baskets. Mother told us that she wanted to head out to the village for a little visit after our people returned home. This was quite unusual. In fact, I could not recall her ever visiting the village prior to this occasion. I'm not sure what inspired her to want to make a call on the slaves. It was inexplicable and downright bizarre. Uncle Robert and I exchanged quizzical looks, but we both knew better than to question Mother once she had decided on a course of action.

About forty-five minutes later we heard our people coming up the drive and passing the main house. Covey and Lizzie entered the kitchen through the back door surprised to see the baskets. They had never seen Mother prepare food before. I have to admit, neither had I! Mother explained to them her intentions in heading to the village, and they immediately offered to run to the cabins and get some people to cart the food but Mother waved off the suggestion, saying that between the six of us, we should have no trouble toting the baskets. Shortly thereafter Covey, Lizzie, Uncle Robert and I had our hands full carrying the baskets of bread, chicken, biscuits, and preserves, down the lane. Mother trod along with us, each of her hands occupied with that of my cousins. Together we traveled past the grove of maples and pines toward the cluster of huts. Our people were all aflutter in their little village. The young ones were running about and most of the adults were conversing near the big oak.

Our arrival caused quite a shock. Of course we were received warmly, particularly Mother, who rarely had any contact with our people other than Covey and Lizzie. Yet I caught a hint, *just a hint*, of disappointment. I remember wondering if perhaps they felt that we had intruded on their private time. Though all of our hands were of course our property, tradition dictated that Saturday afternoon and Sunday belonged to them. Perhaps it was only my imagination.

Mother was quickly offered a seat as Cicero ran off to grab a rocker from his porch. They were also quite excited at the bounty we had brought, and the womenfolk threw out a blanket, and set about arranging the food.

Cicero got his banjo and began to play. Ellen, Eliza and Lizzie began to dance, and were joined by Jacob and Harriet. Ulysses and Penny took seats nearby and clapped along with the tune. As the festivities began, I observed Uncle Robert pull Bartholomew aside. The two talked quietly, and then walked over to Jeremy's cabin. Curious, I tagged along behind. Uncle Robert rapped on Jeremy's door, but there was no answer. After a dozen seconds had passed, Uncle Robert pushed open the door. I forced my head between the two men to see that the cabin was empty.

We went back to the big oak and partook of the food and cider, and had a very nice time. I had wandered through our people's gatherings before, but had never really been a part of one. They were certainly ignorant, there was to be no discussion of Greek philosophy or political dissertation. I could see that Mother was a bit uneasy and detached, but she was certainly entertained by their jovial manner and congenial nature. They were like children; but nice, pleasant children. Uncle Robert even participated in a game of horseshoes with Zeke, Jacob and Bartholomew. It was during this game that Uncle Robert's attention became diverted. I noticed that he was looking past the village toward the path that led toward the creek. Following his

43

gaze I ascertained what had drawn his interest. Walking up the path, carrying a fishing pole and a stringer of three fish, was Jeremy.

Jeremy was bounding along quite happily, when he suddenly froze in place. He was too far away for me to see his face, but I could imagine the look of confused fear that must have contorted his features when he noticed Uncle Robert in the village. After about fifteen seconds or so Jeremy resumed his approach but this time his stride was much altered. Now he trod slowly, staggering occasionally. Bartholomew had also caught sight of Jeremy and briskly came over to Uncle Robert.

"Oh he too sick for church, huh?" I go get de whip from de barn Massa, I take care of him!"

"Hold on now Bartholomew, it's the Sabbath. We'll have no whippings today. Let me speak with you a minute." Uncle Robert handed me his horseshoe and took Bartholomew off to one side. I couldn't hear what he was saying, but I watched the familiar smirk cross his face and saw Bartholomew shake his head in affirmation and let out a hearty laugh.

Uncle Robert returned to the game. Jeremy continued to feign illness, staggering, and contorting his face. He came up to us holding his stomach with his free hand, and tried to hand the stringer of fish to my uncle.

"Ohhhh!" the slave moaned. "Hallo Massa. I taught dat maybe I go catch you some catfish."

"No thank you Jeremy," my uncle said as he made his throw. "I think maybe you could use them in your weakened state." I would have expected a grin to accompany this remark, but my uncle's face remained deadpan.

"Ohhhh." moaned the field hand, continuing his unconvincing act. "Dat awful nice of you, Massa." As Jeremy put on his charade, he was glancing hungrily past us toward the bounty of food on the blankets. He took a step toward the victuals when Uncle Robert stepped in front of him.

"Now Jeremy, I think you've already over-exerted yourself. It's off to bed with you. Bartholomew! Come here please. Help old Jeremy here to his cabin, and get him right to bed."

Jeremy opened his mouth to argue with this idea, but thought better of it. He dejectedly moped toward his cabin, not waiting for Bartholomew. During the remainder of the afternoon, I saw his cabin door crack open occasionally as he looked longingly toward the festivities.

About three o'clock we gathered ourselves up and prepared to head for home. Uncle Robert called Jacob over, gave him a pass, and instructed him to take Penny back to Deep Dene before nightfall. We then began the stroll back to the house. To this day I don't know what prompted my mother to set up the picnic. My best guess would be that she wanted to see the interaction between Ulysses and his wife, but I have no real evidence of this. It is pure speculation. As we rounded the grove of maples and pines I listened as Mother and Uncle Robert discussed Jeremy. Not all masters insisted that their people attend church, and Uncle Robert was a bit ambivalent about the issue. Mother disapproved of Jeremy missing the service, professing equal fear for his soul and of the impression his absence made on the other White families. Uncle Robert appeared to be more vexed at the slave's deceitfulness than at anything else. Mother asked him if he intended to let the punishment stand at missing the picnic. My uncle shook his head.

"That stupid fool might actually think that I believed his story if I confined his punishment to that. No, I have something else in mind. Bartholomew will take care of it tomorrow."

The following morning I accompanied my uncle to the plantation storehouse where we were met by Zeke and Bartholomew. This was a habitual event, as every Monday we apportioned weekly rations to our people. Uncle Robert unlocked the door to the stone building and we began to distribute the supplies. Each slave was given a peck of corn meal, two and half pounds of bacon, and eight ounces of coffee. Some masters prefer to feed their slaves daily in order to keep tighter reign over them. Others provide daily rations because they are afraid that their slaves are so stupid that they would not economize their food, and like dogs, eat it all right away. We never had any problems like that. Our people's rations always lasted the week, supplemented by their garden plots and other foodstuffs they bought or bartered for in the market. Added to these food supplies were two pair of work clothes Bartholomew was to give to Ulysses.

Zeke and Bartholomew loaded the rations aboard a wagon and took the provisions to the village for distribution. Before they were off, Uncle Robert turned to Bartholomew.

"Did you get Jeremy set up as I instructed?"

"Yas sir, I sure did!" the slave driver laughed. "He wouldn't come out of his cabin 'til I said I was goin' fo de whip, but he be in de field, you'll see!" he and Zeke shared a good chuckle as they drove off.

It took us another quarter hour to reaffix the lids to the barrels, tie the bags, and secure the storehouse, after which time my uncle turned to me with a grin.

"Come out to the field for a bit. I know that you have to attend to your lessons this morning, but I think you'll enjoy a gander at the slaves," he said, winking.

We walked over to the stable and saddled the horses ourselves since the hands were getting their rations and then moving out to the fields. By the time we had trotted out to the field, the slaves had already renewed the potato planting that they had begun on Saturday. As we approached I could see the familiar process; one slave widening the plowed furrow with his hoe, the second deposited the seed potato, and the third closing the hole. However one of the gangs seemed to be different. Ulysses, Jeremy, and Jacob had been working together on Saturday. Despite our distance, I could see that a woman was

46

now helping Ulysses and Jacob. Bartholomew was very methodical, so it seemed odd that the gang had changed. Also, the usual songs of the slaves were not audible; rather I could hear fits of laughter as they worked.

I was trying to discern exactly what was going on. When we had approached sufficiently, the picture (both figuratively and literally) came into focus. The woman with Ulysses and Jacob *was* Jeremy! He was wearing a dress and kerchief. I glanced at my uncle (who was riding alongside me) and was met with a wide grin.

We pulled up next to Bartholomew, who was of course directing the entire operation with his characteristic authority. However, the usually stoic driver wore a smirk of his own. From this vantage point I could see Jeremy's unhappy expression, and could almost feel the indignation radiating from him. My uncle made no more mention of the slave's attire, but confined his conversation with Bartholomew to agrarian matters.

Masters differ in their methods for punishing slaves. Colonel Jeffers advocates whipping, and uses the lash liberally to enforce his rules. I know Mr. Whistler used the stocks, forcing an offender to stand for long periods locked in the pillory. Luckily, my uncle did not have to inflict punishment often. I had seen him slap a slave on occasion, but he had a real distaste for physical abuse. I'm sure he realized that the more draconian methods of other masters where in large part counterproductive since the injury incurred with flogging, or the duration of display in the stocks, removed a worker from the fields. But, I still believe that his primary aversion to these forms of punishment originated from his personal dislike of ill-treatment.

So Jeremy was forced to endure the emasculating ridicule of tilling the fields in women's clothing. He not only received mockery from the other male slaves, but the women joined in too. Unfortunately for Jeremy the story was circulated to other plantations as well, and when he did attend church again, or the market, he was subjected to jibes from other colored folk. As unconventional as my uncle's maneuver may have been, the day that boy spent dressed as a woman must have worked. Jeremy never again missed church. I even remember him attending once when he had a bad case of sour stomach. He must have run to the outhouse ten times during service that Sunday. Judging from the way he walked home, he may have even shit his pants.

A few weeks after the Jeremy incident my uncle pulled me aside and told me that he and Mother were discussing my prospects as future owner of The Copper Beeches. They had concluded that I should have a broader perspective on the means and methods of running a plantation. According to my mother, my experiences had primarily been limited to the techniques and ideas of my uncle and father and in order for me to make critical decisions on how *I* would run the plantation, I should broaden my horizons. Now there are some that would consider a lad of my age too young to trouble with such ideas, but you must remember that I was considered exceptionally bright and also that my mother was always contemplating means to expand my education. In our rural locale, she placed much emphasis on book learning, but was sensible enough to realize that I would need a practical education as well if I were to be a planter. It turned out that that Uncle Robert had gotten permission from Colonel Jeffers for me to spend a week at Chiltern Grange.

I was less than thrilled with the prospect. I liked the Colonel and his family well enough, but I had never been away from home before and also much preferred to spend my time reading and studying rather then attending to plantation duties. However, I never argued with Mother or Uncle Robert and the pragmatist in me concluded that their idea was valid. I should indeed expose myself to other perspectives if I hoped to make intelligent decisions on our own plantation. After all, being an owner is a tremendous responsibility. Not only are there a plethora of aspects to farming, but management, fiscal matters, and commerce all had to be considered. Added to these duties was the fact that it would be my responsibility to provide for and protect not only the Covingtons, but also "our people." In essence, our family numbered twenty all of whom currently depended on Uncle Robert, but they would eventually have to look to me.

I took some solace in the fact that there had been other intellectual Virginians who were both planters and thinkers. Both Thomas Jefferson and James Madison bridged the gap between agrarian and academic, though I hoped that I could manage my affairs better than the third President since he outspent his income, accruing huge debt. Regardless, the following morning I packed a bag and prepared to head to Chiltern Grange.

Zeke was given the task of driving me to the Jeffers plantation. He had of course secured a pass from Uncle Robert, since he would have to return alone. I bid farewell to Mother, Uncle Robert, the girls, and Covey and Lizzie. As we rode down the drive I recall looking back at our house. I tried not to; I didn't want them to think that I was scared or uneasy. Yet my gaze was magnetically pulled in that direction. I did have a certain degree of trepidation, but this was tempered with the odd sense of responsibility that would one day be mine. I had never really given it much thought until recently. The women were reentering the house as I proudly surveyed that structure. I saw Uncle Robert strolling toward the stable. I could see the barn with the slaves hurrying about their duties before heading to the fields. As we reached the crest of the small hill before turning onto the road, my last sight was of the grove of maples and pines and the few wisps of smoke that drifted above their peaks from the village beyond.

About a half an hour after leaving The Copper Beeches, Zeke and I came across a pair of patrollers. Those who act as patrollers are a varied lot. The largest planters would never belittle themselves by riding patrol, but the small-scale farmers, even those without slaves, were active in this duty. Overseers, planters' sons, and general ruffians all took their turn patrolling the roads for runaway slaves. As we approached, I could see that the two men on horseback were trailing a Negro whose hands were tied and tethered to one's saddle. I was a bit concerned when I got a closer look at these individuals. They were a couple of brutes. Their clothes were worn and dusty and their faces and hands covered in dirt.

"Hold up there, boy!" one yelled to Zeke, brandishing a shotgun.

Zeke pulled the team to a stop and set the brake.

"Where you goin', boy?" the man questioned, waving the shotgun in Zeke's face.

Zeke did not fluster at the patroller's attempts at intimidation, but merely turned to me and said, "Maybe you bes splain to dem, sir."

I have to admit, I wasn't as cool as Zeke. I knew that many of these illiterate, downtrodden rogues resented the more well-to-do and I thought they might not be too congenial to a lad like myself.

"Ahhem," I cleared my throat, "I am Gideon Covington, and I am heading to Chiltern Grange, the plantation of Colonel Jeffers."

"Covington? James Covington's boy?" the other asked.

"Yes, James was my father," I replied.

The patroller turned to his companion with the shotgun. "James Covington—Captain Covington. He served with Daddy in Mexico. You remember the story… how the company fought in Guadelupe?"

"Oh yeah, yeah." A glimmer of recollection crossed the dirty face.

"I be Jack McCormick and this here's my brother Avery. Our Daddy fought with your Daddy in Mexico!"

During this exchange I peered behind the two men at the slave in tow. He stood silent, swaying back and forth, unable to maintain his balance. He was obviously exhausted as his chest was also heaving. He had bruises on his face and a bloody lip. He also had a nasty gash on his temple, probably from the butt of the shotgun.

It appeared Jack McCormick was beaming in anticipation of my recognizing his father's name, (which I didn't) but I diverted the conversation to their prisoner.

"What do you have there, a runaway?"

The brothers were roused by my query, as they had apparently forgotten about their prize. "Oh. Yeah, this here is a runaway. I guess." Avery laughed, nudging his brother. He says he belongs to a feller named Crosley, but he ain't got no pass. We're gonna take him into Fincastle and see if anybody claims him."

I had never heard of anyone named "Crosley" and I did not recognize the Negro either. I was, however concerned about his injuries. Patrollers commonly abused their catches. Captured slaves were not *their* property after all, so they were not overly concerned about their welfare. This was particularly true of non-slave owners. They often used the opportunity to brutalize the only caste lower than themselves. Uncle Robert is of the opinion that their abuse was not really directed at the slaves, but as resentment toward their masters. I'm not sure if this is true, but I have to admit I was impressed at Uncle Robert's analysis, given his usual aloof, detached nature.

"I suppose he tried to fight with you," I inquired coyly.

"Well you know how these niggers are. They understand best when the message is sent good and clear. I used to work as an overseer and I always set the tone early on as to who's in charge. That way I had less trouble later."

51

I wanted to explain to these crackers that this Mr. Crosley might not approve of his property being abused needlessly. However, given my youth, I did not venture into censuring these two men who though my social inferior, were chronologically superior and thus due a modicum of respect.

In the course of this conversation I had accrued some degree of confidence. I'm not sure if it was their apparent respect for my father, or some internal fortitude, but when I addressed them again it was in a more forceful manner.

"Please take a good look at my man, here. His name is Zeke Covington. He will be returning to our plantation alone. He has a pass, but I want to make sure that he is not confused as being a runaway. I would appreciate it if you could tell any other patrollers you come across on the way to Fincastle that he is not to be molested."

I thought that the brothers might be angered by my direct nature, but they seemed impressed with my discourse. "Zeke Covington. Okay. Will do. You have a good trip now."

With that the McCormicks continued on their way, dragging their prisoner along behind. I noticed that his breathing had eased a bit. I was glad that perhaps the delay we imposed allowed him to rest a spell.

When we were out of earshot from the brothers, Zeke said, "I's sure glad you told dem paddyrollers 'bout me. (for some reason the Negroes always call patrollers "paddyrollers") Dey sure beat dat boy silly. I don't knows him. He may be a runaway, but I sure don't wants to end up lookin' like him! You sure did handle dem well, Massa Gidin'," Zeke laughed. "You jus' a boy an you already commandin' respect. You gonna make a fine planter one day."

I was bolstered by Zeke's vote of confidence. I had always been introverted and quiet, and to this day I generally do not enjoy interaction with others. However, I was part of the patrician class and as such had to learn to exert my authority.

52

Eventually we arrived at Chiltern Grange. I had been to the Jeffers place before, but not for a few years, and I had been too young to remember much of its physical features. The estate sat well back from the main road and two large stone pillars marked the entrance to the private drive. Zeke directed the team between the pillars and as we drove the remaining half-mile to the house, I surveyed the surroundings. The beginning of the drive was heavily wooded and the dirt road traveled straight for three hundred yards before turning abruptly to the left. After the turn, the woods were left behind, exposing the gently rolling hills of the plantation, which were silhouetted by the mountains a few miles to the west.

The house's architecture was a frontier attempt at eastern Virginian style. The homes of the tidewater region were constructed of quarried stone and expensive brick laid by experienced masons where the style emulated Greek and Roman design. In the Shenandoah Valley, we had little access to cut stone, and made due with the building materials of the area. The foundation of the Jeffers' home was constructed of bricks baked on the premises. Such a foundation was typical in our area, but unlike others these bricks had been whitewashed. The main structure was built of wood, with huge carved wooden columns that were facsimiles of the type Corinthian pillars used in the finer eastern plantations. The whole of the house, like the foundation, had been painted white to disguise the building material. In hearing this description, one might think this attempt at deception made for an ungainly, transparent reproduction, but quite the converse is true. It was a handsome building, distinctive and stately. The house sat atop a small hill or mound, and its ascendancy commanded the respect of the numerous outbuildings and distant slave village.

The Jeffers plantation was larger than ours and the Colonel owned approximately thirty to forty slaves. His crops were as diversified as ours, but he put a greater emphasis on tobacco (probably in an attempt to akin himself to the easterners), and also on the lucrative cattle market. I suspect that the Colonel would have preferred to concentrate solely on cash-crop agriculture, but in our part of the state that would have amounted to economic ruin. As we continued down the drive I could see specks on the hillside moving about like ants. It became apparent that the "ants" were the slaves busy at their work. I could also see one man among them on horseback. Undoubtedly this was the Colonel's eldest son Winston, who acted as overseer.

When we pulled up in front of the broad steps of the front porch, a house slave dressed extravagantly in ruffles came running up to grab my bag. A moment later the Colonel stepped onto the porch accompanied by Mrs. Jeffers.

"Hello there, Gideon!" he boomed.

"Hello, sir." I returned, awkwardly shaking his hand. I had already removed my hat at the sight of Mrs. Jeffers, and bowed slightly in her direction.

"What a polite young man. Have you eaten? Can I have Emma fix you something?" the gracious hostess asked.

"No thank you, I'm fine ma'am." I replied.

"Carmichael," the Colonel turned his attention to the house servant, "put young Master Covington's bag in the blue room," (as it turned out, each room in the house was painted a different color and the inhabitants of the structure called each room by its tone) "and then run out to the stable and bring Champion and a mount for our guest."

"Go on now Zeke. Get back home. Thank you for the ride," I said, ushering the slave off.

"Good Lord boy, no need to be so polite to a nigger! Well that's why you're here isn't it? We'll fix you right up!" the Colonel jibed.

54

"Why don't you show Mr. Covington around the house while you're waiting for Carmichael?" Mrs. Covington directed her husband.

"Fine idea," he said, kissing his wife's hand in demonstrative fashion.

We entered the house and Mrs. Jeffers disappeared to her sitting room where she had been working on some needlepoint, while the Colonel gave me a grand tour of the house from top to bottom. It was a large house, and I remember that I was surprised that they had been able to find adequate shades for delineating a distinct color for each room.

Though the home was large, it seemed quite full. The Colonel had three sons, the eldest being the aforementioned Winston, who was twenty years of age, though the next two were much younger. Zachary was three, and Mitchell was one. There were four house servants: Carmichael, Emma the cook, a maid called Rachel, and a nursemaid for the children named Mary.

After showing me the house, came a tour of the plantation. Exiting the large double front doors, we found Carmichael waiting attentively with the Colonel's horse and a second mount. We saddled up and the Colonel led the way, as we headed off behind the house.

I liked the Colonel. He was prideful and arrogant, but was at heart a nice man. He began by giving an exposition on the history of his family lineage, which he claimed could be traced to English royalty. He then discussed how his great-great-grandfather had had the foresight to petition the colonial governor for a land grant in the western part Virginia. According to the Colonel, his ancestor had known that the Shenandoah Valley was fertile and that Virginia could only become "the brightest jewel in the colonies" if its inhabitants were to expand westward. There had been whispers that the first Jeffers in the valley had not been the recipient of the governor's patronage, but rather had been a squatter fleeing indentured servitude. However, no one would have dared to insinuate such to the Colonel, as it would have unquestionably been answered with a challenge to a duel.

We rode past the springhouse and the kitchen garden, which were conveniently close to the house. Next we came to the stables, the hog and cattle pens, and the hen house. Adjacent to the stables was a small blacksmithing area. Further away from the house were the smokehouse and the barn for storing and drying tobacco, and the granary. Next to the granary was the storehouse. From here we rode a considerable distance to the village. Despite the immaculate condition of the main house and its periphery structures, the slave village was somewhat dilapidated. Our people's cabins were in much better shape. Of course there were more slaves at Chiltern Grange so the village was larger than our own, but the cabins were mere shacks. Few had windows, and a couple even had thatch roofs. The twenty or so shanties were situated in a complete circle, at the center of which stood a solitary post with a thick iron ring affixed about eight feet up.

"This is of course where we keep our niggers," the Colonel boasted turning his horse in a panoramic sweep.

I recall that I was appalled, but I can't recollect if it was at the horrific conditions of the village, or the Colonel's pride in the dilapidated housing. We did not tally long at the village, but proceeded on to the fields. The field that was being worked was a considerable distance from the village; and it took us a good ten minutes to reach the hillside being farmed. As we approached I could see Winston Jeffers, his back to us, directing the slaves from horseback. He patrolled back and forth in a sentry-like manner as the slaves toiled before him. As we drew closer, it looked as if there were four gangs of ten or so, and I noticed that even very young children were hard at work. When we were fifty yards away, Winston caught sight of us and galloped over in our direction.

"Hello, son!" the Colonel beamed to his protégé.

"G'morning, sir," Winston returned tipping his broad brimmed hat respectfully. "I see you have our young squire with you, huh? Well we'll be sure to learn him how things work at the largest plantation in Botetourt County!"

I'm not sure if this boast was technically accurate, but it revealed that primogeniture had carried the Colonel's pride to his eldest son. I did of course already know Winston, but not personally. He was a short young man, standing little more than five feet tall. He had the same jet-black hair as the Colonel, but his locks were curly like his mother's. His face was very distinctive; I dare say "ugly." Both his parents were quite handsome, but Winston had an exceptionally large head that appeared too big for his body. He had hazel eyes, like the Colonel, but large bushy eyebrows, the origin of which I have no idea. His nose was particularly unattractive as it was large and bulbous. Of particular interest was that Winston carried a shotgun on his saddle, next to which was affixed a bullwhip.

It is not unusual for a son who has yet to earn his inheritance to work as an overseer. Many felt that such a duty gave important training in plantation management. This training was thought to be essential, as they would eventually take over operations. This arrangement did have certain drawbacks though, since a professional overseer would have more experience in handling slaves. However this shortcoming was usually outweighed by the fact that the vocational overseer could not always be trusted and their duty at controlling the slaves often put them in conflict with owners who of course maintained ultimate control. Often overseers would be countermanded by owners, which undermined them in front of the slaves and diluted their effectiveness. Also, a member of the family would be less likely to abuse his father's property (property that would also one day be his).

"Well, I'm going to leave you here with Winston for awhile. I'll see you back at the house later." With that the Colonel gave me a friendly pat on the back and went trotting off upon his prized steed.

CHAPTER 4

Looking past Winston I could see that the slaves were unloading tobacco seedlings from several wagons and carefully planting them in the field they had cultivated out of the hillside.

"You see Gideon," Winston began his tutorial, "We burned the grass off this field a month ago. This helps sterilize the soil and also kills any bugs that might be lurking underneath. After that was done we fertilized it with manure. We plowed it several times since then, and used a peg-tooth harrow to break up the soil even more. Meanwhile the seedlings had been growing closer to the Grange." He motioned with his shotgun in the general direction of the house. "When you plant the seeds for the seedlings, you have to cover them with branches and such in order to protect them from frost. Now if you look at the seedlings you'll notice that they are about ten inches in height. I prefer that they reach a foot before planting, but the Colonel consulted the almanac and insisted that they be planted now."

I already knew all about tobacco seedlings from Bartholomew, but I did not want to offend Winston, especially since he was apparently quite proud of his acumen on the subject.

He continued, "'Baccy is a fragile plant. Most think it's hardy since it depletes the soil so quickly, but it really ain't; especially in this part of the state. In the valley, we have to take special care or we'll never yield a profit. As you can see, I have one gang using pegs to create the holes for the plants, another planting, and yet another doing the transporting from the seed beds."

"Do you top and suckle the plants?" I asked, intent on demonstrating that I had some knowledge on the subject.

Winston did a double take, obviously surprised by the query. "Well now, that's a right good question. When these plants reach a height of two or three feet-- I prefer two, we'll lop off the top portion. You see it's the *leaves* that we want to receive the plant's energy. The money is in these leaves." He pulled a piece of dried tobacco from his inside pocket and stroked the brown material, silently punctuating his point. "Of course after the plant is topped, new shoots will start growing at the base of where it was cut. We don't want the plant to use its energy growing new shoots, the energy's got to go to the leaves!" He shook the dried leave for emphasis as he said this. "So the new shoots will have to be cut as well."

"Now one thing you've got to know about 'baccy,'" he continued. "Worms love it. If you don't pay attention, worms will eat your whole crop. I always make sure the our people do an inspection every other day to make sure we don't have any worms. But, I'll tell you a secret..." he leaned close to me even though there was no one within earshot of us. "...I bring guinea hens out of the coop and let them roam around out here. They love to eat the worms as much as the worms love to eat the 'baccy! I tell you one guinea hen on patrol is worth three niggers inspecting!"

Now this was hardly a revelation. At The Copper Beeches, special effort did not have to be made to bring guinea hens out to the fields. Hens and turkeys roamed all over our plantation protecting all of our crops from insects, not just the tobacco.

"While we're on the subject of 'baccy, I might as well tell you about the harvesting, since you won't be here when we do that. We will harvest the crop in late August or early September. Now this here variety is called "bright-leaf" and it takes a trained eye to know when it's ready to be cut. I can't show you since it's not time, but I'll see if I can describe it to you," he said, adjusting the hat upon his disproportionately large head. "The leaves will have small spots on them and the end of the leaf will

60

be curled. Now as I said, this will occur somewhere between late August and early September. We'll carefully count out a number of small curved knives and give them to the hands to split each plant from the top down to three inches above the bottom. Then we cut off the entire plant below the split, turn it upside down and put them between the rows. A second gang will collect these stalks and place them on tobacco sticks. We cut our sticks four feet long so that they can hold seven or eight stalks each."

"Listen," he wagged a finger in my face. "Now I told you that we *carefully* count out those knives. You have to be very, very attentive to this. Remember that Nat Turner business. That was twenty years ago but that runaway got fifty slaves to help him slaughter seventy whites. There's nothing as dangerous as a nigger with a weapon. Two years ago one of the knives came up missing. Like I said, I count them *carefully*. I had to beat the tar out of ten of them one at a time before I found the one that took it. Of course he said that he lost it in the field, but you can't trust a word one of those Black devils tells you. I found it in his cabin. Now I wanted to kill him outright, but the Colonel made me give him thirty lashes instead. Between you and me, I never was good at keeping track of stripes on a nigger's back!" (Yet, he could carefully count knives. I suppose his mathematical abilities came and went.) He chuckled and nudged me with his elbow. "I can't rightly say how many lashes I put on that darkie, but it was enough to kill him just the same."

He seemed almost giddy at recollecting how he had basically murdered the slave. I remember thinking that it may have been necessary to whip the boy, but to kill him? Winston kept telling me what was economically smart, but it wasn't too smart to destroy one's property. I suppose an example had to be set, but if he had just beat his face in he could have still sold him and not lost the value of the slave.

I was stirred from this thought as Winston continued his lesson. "Now I'm sure that you are aware that 'baccy must be cured. There are some that sell their 'baccy right to a wholesaler, who does the curing, but that takes away from the profits. A smart planter cures his own tobacco. Behind the hog pen, over yonder is the curing barn. Can you see it?" he pointed again with the gun.

"Yes…Yes. I see it."

"Well, this here bright-leaf 'baccy is flue cured. There's a brick furnace in the barn, and the furnace has a metal flue. This flue circulates the hot air to cure the 'baccy that is hanging inside. You see the sticks are put on poles that stretch across the eaves. They hang from one side of the barn to the other. Once it's all filled, we light a fire in the furnace and let it burn for a few days. Now you have to keep the fire stoked mind you. When they're done curing they'll be yellow. Then you have to open the doors to let a little moisture back into the leaves."

"On an eastern plantation they'd next be moved to a pack house where the leaves would be sorted, bundled, and taken to market. Unfortunately out west here, it would be too expensive for us to do all that. We let Drower over in Fincastle store it until the agent comes from Richmond. He brings a dozen slaves with him and sorts it and transports it back east."

No sooner had Winston finished this little discourse than he sprang into a fit of rage and galloped off about twenty-five yards where a slave had stopped at a wagon for a drink of water. "Hey you! Boy! What's you're name? Jackson isn't it?" he yelled. The slave cowered. Much to my dread Winston tore loose the bullwhip from his saddle, swung it about his head, and snapped it to its full length letting out a thunderous "crack!" Luckily he didn't hit the poor fellow. The boy scurried back to his work begging forgiveness as he sprinted.

Winston trotted back to me. "That water has to last all day. If I let every one drink when they wanted, they'd drink it all

62

down in ten minutes. Plus-- remember this Gideon—you can't trust niggers. They are the laziest bunch on this planet. If you don't put the fear of God into them, they'll lounge around all day. If I let that boy drink, before you know it, every darkie out here would suddenly say they were parched and not get a lick of work done!"

I was horrified that he was ready to whip a slave just for getting a drink of water. Yet, there was sense in what he said. Our people were afraid of Bartholomew, and that's why they worked. Granted, Uncle Robert treated them kindly, but his generosity is not what motivated them to labor for us, it was the fear of punishment or sale down river.

Over the next several days I traveled the grounds with Winston. I saw very little of the Colonel or Mrs. Jeffers, except in the evening. We all ate dinner together and spent time in the parlor afterward. I was used to intellectual discourse in our own parlor, but this was hardly the case at the Jeffers. I did enjoy Mrs. Jeffers singing and renditions on the harpsichord, but I had to turn to the books I'd brought for any real cerebral stimulation.

Winston showed me everything on the plantation and was very thorough in his tutorial. There was a great deal that I already knew, but also a lot that I did not. My mother and uncle were correct in saying that I would get a different perspective at Chiltern Grange. There were marked differences between the methods used at the Jeffers' place and those we employed at The Copper Beeches. Of course their plantation was larger than our own, which in itself necessitated some different means, but there were also other differences in agricultural technique and custom. Some of these were better than our own, some worse, but it was of value to be able to experience and evaluate the differences. The greatest dissimilarity however was in the area of labor management.

Winston was a harsh overseer. He not only punished his slaves ruthlessly, he was vicious in his very disposition toward

63

them. The plantation's slaves universally feared him. I know that Winston (and I suppose the Colonel) felt that his methods were necessary, and fruitful for the plantation, but in comparing them with those of Uncle Robert I believe my uncle had the better idea. I suppose that an individual's general disposition has much to do with the way they treat their people. Winston was ornery by nature and exulted in his role as overseer. Conversely, Uncle Robert was a kind man who exercised authority only out of necessity. I often felt that he would have been happier had my father lived to run things at The Copper Beeches. Had this been the case, he could have taken a less active role in the plantation's management, which I'm sure would have suited him just fine. Regardless, the slaves were like children. Yes, they act inappropriately. Yes, they are lazy. Yes, they try to buck authority. However after watching Winston in action, I concluded that a kind, considerate master who used the whip sparingly was apt to get more out of his people than men like the harsh overseer of Chiltern Grange.

I suppose I solidified this opinion on my third day at the Jeffers place. It was at this time that a teenage boy named Jonas drew the wrath of Master Winston. Winston and I were still supervising the tobacco planting when he asked me if I could keep an eye on things while he went to use the outhouse. He must have felt a bit uneasy about this, because he told me that he would rush right back. I was supervising the hands to the best of my ability, which basically meant looking mean and slowly riding around them. After about an hour I began to get worried. I started casting nervous glances toward the house hoping to see Winston riding back. Though it was about a half mile away, I had a fairly good view of the house since we were still planting on the hillside. However the stable obstructed my view of the outhouse.

The slaves at Chiltern Grange did not sing as they worked like ours did. They toiled in almost absolute silence, which I have to admit was a bit eerie. I was pondering this difference when I finally saw Winston emerge from behind the stable; oddly he was leading his horse by the reins, rather than riding him. It was a great distance, but I also perceived an odd "waddle" in his gait. He next led his horse inside the stable, and emerged with a different horse, which he led by the reins to the adjacent barn. This situation greatly intrigued me. I wondered almost aloud about what could be the cause of this peculiar circumstance. Ten minutes later, he emerged again, though this time he was riding in a buggy.

It took Winston quite some time to reach me, and he had to park the buggy a good piece away from where we were working due to the incline of the hillside. Winston's peculiar stride was more evident now as he ambled over.

"Are you alright?" I asked, much concerned.

"Well, I hope so," he replied with a wince.

Now I had prepared myself for an explanation along the lines of diarrhea, or some such ailment, but much to my surprise this was not the case.

Winston reluctantly explained, "I was in a hurry to do my business and get back up here. I know these niggers try to take advantage of any opportunity to slack off, so I was trying to make it quick. Well, in my haste I neglected to use the whip…"

I am not sure if this is true of all parts of the country, but in Virginia, every outhouse is equipped with a "spider whip." This is merely a switch or branch that one sticks into the hole and makes a quick swirl before setting their backsides down. This is particularly needed as the weather warms up. Flies and other insects are attracted to the odor from the outhouse, which in turn causes spiders to spin webs in the hole. More than one person has received a nasty spider bite when trying to take a shit.

"He got me right on the pecker."

I let out an audible gasp at this revelation.

65

"Right away it swelled up. I ran to the house and had Emma take a look. She thinks the spider was a brown recluse. She put a poultice of wet tobacco on it and said I have to keep it on there, so it's wrapped around it with twine."

I was horrified at this development, but not everyone was. Unfortunately, this slave named Jonas overheard the conversation and let out an *almost* inaudible snicker. I say almost, because it did not escape Winston's ear. He flew into a violent rage. I thought it lucky that he was not too mobile at the moment, as he could not reach the slave before he scurried back to the row and began hoeing vigorously. This however, did not save him. Winston brought the entire operation to a halt. He made all of the slaves lie down their tools and march to the village. He said not a word to me, but climbed aboard the buggy and rode off toward the slave quarters. I awkwardly followed, full of trepidation.

Once all of the slaves had assembled, Winston ordered Jonas to the whipping post in the center of the village and had two other slaves bind his hands to the ring at the top of the post. Though I do not believe that Jonas had ever been whipped before, it was obvious to that he had witnessed other such displays at this same spot, as he was crying and begging like a little girl.

As for myself, this was the first time that I had ever been present for a flogging. I had seen Bartholomew punch and slap a few of our boys, and even saw Uncle Robert give Jeremy a whack in the face with a riding crop, but this was the first time I witnessed such severe corporal punishment.

Every slave on the plantation knew what was expected. They all had gathered in a wide circle around the post, forced to watch the brutalization. I recall scanning their faces as they stood in anticipation of the event. The older slaves, both men and women, were stoic. Their faces were expressionless. The children however were crying and clutching at their mother's

66

skirts. As Winston began to deliver the blows, the elderly remained emotionless. They stared with dead eyes as the lash fell. Those in their twenties down to the teens grimaced and winced with each stripe, and the children continued to cry.

Jonas let loose bloodcurdling cries with each stroke, whimpering in between. The stripes and welts quickly began to appear on his back. Shortly these would be replaced with open cuts. Soon he was reduced to begging. "Do Massa! Do Massa!" he would say between stripes. (This puzzled me as it seemed to make no sense. I later found out that for some inexplicable reason, this was a common expression for slaves to utter as they were flogged. "I be a good nigger! Massa!" "Have mercy on a poor nigger Massa!" were among his other cries.

After thirty, he hung limp by his arms. However, Winston gave him ten more nonetheless. He had given no address before he began, and neither did he do so afterward. He merely glared at Jonas. Then he slowly rotated himself, panned his glare at all of the slaves. Finally he ordered them back to work, though he told two male slaves to drag Jonas to his cabin and directed a negress named Rebecca to tend to his wounds.

This display of brutality affected me greatly. I felt there was no need to be so harsh with this boy, and additionally, it was an example of poor management. I know that Winston believed that asserting his authority kept his slaves in line and thus kept them working hard. However, by allowing his temper to get the better of him, he had lost an hour's worth of work from the slaves since they had been forced to abandon their planting to witness the punishment. Also, he lost Jonas for at least a week, and Rebecca for some time too. This was hardly an efficient use of manpower.

Winston told me later that he administered the extra ten stripes because niggers "were tricky" and would pretend to faint before they actually passed out. I suppose this is plausible, but that Jonas surely looked unconscious to me.

67

The day following the whipping I was at the stable preparing to mount up to ride out to the field when Carmichael, the house servant came running out to get me.

"Massa Covin'ton! Massa Covin'ton!"

"Yes Carmichael?" I arrested my assent, one foot still in the stirrup.

"You'se needed at de house. Come right away!"

I tried to query further, but the houseboy was off again before I could utter another word. I handed the reigns to the slave who had been assisting me and ambled back toward the mansion puzzling over the strange interruption. As I rounded the corner of the house I was amazed to see Zeke sitting in our buggy and Colonel Jeffers standing on the front porch, his hat in his hands.

"Gideon," he said softly, walking over to me and putting his arm around my shoulder, "word has come that your mother is ill. Your uncle has sent this boy to take you back to The Copper Beeches."

The news hit me like a cascade of ice water. I was in shock. I said nothing, and simply stared at the Colonel's kind face. He averted his eyes from my gaze, which upon later reflection, should have concerned me deeply. He was a strong, dominant man, and for him to take such a submissive posture should have alerted me that the situation was serious.

The appearance of Carmichael brought me out of my daze. He emerged on the porch carrying my sack.

"Here," the Colonel said taking the satchel from the slave and handing it to me, "I had Carmichael collect your things. It's been a pleasure having you here. You're a fine young man. You will be in our prayers."

I climbed aboard the buggy and we were off. I sat in silence until we had made it onto the road. In retrospect I find it odd that I waited so long to speak to Zeke. I cannot recall if I was still in shock or merely afraid that if I spoke, my voice would waiver from distress. Regardless, the slave waited until addressed before speaking to me.

"What is it Zeke?" I asked solemnly.

"Its de milk sickness." he said quietly.

Milk sickness had taken many lives before, and my mother's survival was by no means guaranteed. At the time, no one was sure what caused the ailment. Now, the general consensus is that it originates with white snakeroot. Cattle that graze on the plant seem to poison their milk, and anyone that drinks that milk, runs the risk of contracting the illness.

"How sick is she?" I asked, trying to keep my voice steady.

"Well, it come on two days ago. Covey thought maybe she be okay, but it got worse. She powerful sick last night. Dat why Massa Robert tell me to come git you."

This illness was not only potentially deadly, but it also inflicted hideous suffering. The afflicted was cursed with extreme nausea and vomiting, and a dreadful weakness caused not only by the dehydration, but also by a slowing of the pulse and respiration. A whitish coating appeared on the tongue and the extremities grew to be as cold as ice.

I relate these conditions because the reader of this manuscript may be unfamiliar with the symptoms of this terrible disorder, but at the time I did not dare to think about the manner in which my mother might be anguishing.

The ride back to The Copper Beeches that day seemed insufferably long, yet I refrained from ordering Zeke to quicken the pace. I had an odd desire for procrastination. I was conflicted between wanting to rush to my mother's side, and an aversion to seeing her in such a state. I'm not sure how long it actually took to return home, nor what I thought about on the ride. I recall that Zeke and I did not converse; yet what went through my mind on that trip has long since faded from my memory.

As we rode up the drive, I saw that the field hands were all milling about the front of the house. Neither Uncle Robert, nor my cousins were in sight. My heart sank at this picture. It was not a good sign that the slaves were not working in the fields. Zeke pulled up in front of the porch and set the brake. My energy returned and I hurriedly leapt from the buggy, but before my foot hit the first step of the porch Covey emerged from the front door.

With tears in her eyes she said quietly, "She gone."

Immediately the female slaves began to wail in despair, some falling to the ground. The male slaves were equally distraught, though less flamboyant in their display of sorrow.

The news hit me like a thunderbolt. I stood frozen in position with one foot resting on the step. Eventually Covey came over and put her arm around me and led me into the house. The girls were in the kitchen with Lizzie. They were quiet, but not crying. I had drawn the conclusion that they did not yet know the news. Covey led me up the stairs. She did not say a word, but very lovingly rubbed my back as we walked.

The door to the bedroom was ajar and I put my hand on it to push it open, but it felt like it was made of lead. The muscles of my arm felt as pliable as a blade of grass and it took intense effort to force the portal inward. As it swung open, I saw Mother lying in the bed, Uncle Robert sitting by her side. In his left hand was that of my mother. In his right was his Bible. His head was bowed, and there were tears in his eyes, but he was not crying. Mother looked pale and ill, but peaceful.

Uncle Robert did not notice my presence until I was standing next to him. Roused from his sorrow, he stood and gave me a hug (this was the first and only time he had ever done so). He patted my back, and then left the room without a word. Covey walked over to the vase by the window and withdrew the wildflowers. She put them on my mother's chest and folded her hands over them.

I sat in the chair vacated by my uncle. Covey left and closed the door behind her. I could hear her sobbing as her footsteps faded down the hall. To this day I regret not spurring Zeke on. Had I hurried, I could have been by her side at her passing. I have seen much death in recent years, some of it quite gruesome. I have lost friends, and watched young boys blown to pieces. I have often recounted battles in my mind and retraced my actions, bemoaning that if I'd fired more accurately, or led in a different manner I might have saved the lives of my comrades. Yet, no regret weighs more heavily upon my mind than not rushing back to The Copper Beeches that day.

My recollections are quite hazy about the events that followed, so I cannot describe with any degree of accuracy how I felt or why I acted as I did. I did not stay by my mother's side very long. I know that some gaze upon the departed and embrace their peacefulness. I however could not bring myself to look at my mother's lifeless body. I have since tried to analyze my feelings and state of mind at that time, but my conclusions are mere speculation. I remember being in sort of a fog. I left my mother without lingering and went to my room where I took up my Bible. I then proceeded down the front stairs where I could hear the girls wailing in the kitchen. I believe that Uncle Robert and Covey were both there trying to console my cousins.

I was desperately in need of solace, yet I wanted to be alone. I felt that I could not endure the grief of others on top of my own. I left via the front door, where old Jack (apparently sensing my sadness) laboriously hoisted himself from his favorite spot and accompanied me as I slowly walked out behind the springhouse. There I sat, resting my back on the cool flagstone wall and opened my Bible. I cannot recount what passages I read that day, but I know that none soothed my pain. I can recall hearing the slaves bustling to and from the house, oblivious to my presence. One thing I do remember quite vividly; I did not shed any tears. Some would conclude that this was due to a

71

sense of manhood. Perhaps even a coming of age. However, upon retrospection I do not believe this to be the case. I was just empty. I felt a hollowness, and I did not logically see how balling could remedy the situation.

The grief I endured over my mother's passing did serve a purpose however. I developed a steely acceptance of death. The scriptures contend that paradise awaits those who have lived a righteous life, and I am apt to agree. However, I became acutely aware that dying is part of living. We will all pass from this earth, and there is nothing that can be done about it, nor can abject sorrow serve any productive purpose. This fact would become implicitly clear in observing the losing battle my uncle would fight against his grief.

My mother's funeral was held at our church in Fincastle. The entire community (both black and white) was in attendance. The service was very nice, and the preacher's sermon very poignant, however the event was excruciating for me. My own sadness was burdensome enough, but to have to endure this collective misery was almost intolerable. The room was so laded with grief that the air itself felt like it weighed upon the congregation. During the service, Uncle Robert stood with Ellen and Eliza on either side of him, his arms around the young girls. They cried into his coat. It appeared to me that the girls were actually supporting him as he swayed unsteadily.

Uncle Robert was never the same. He did not experience a total collapse, but the passing of my mother certainly injured him irreparably. He drank steadily thereafter. He struggled to retain his wit, and his clever jibes became less and less frequent. He continued his duties managing The Copper Beeches, but with little zest or enthusiasm. It was from this change that I became completely aware of his love for my mother. When you are around people for such a large portion of your life, they become part of the scenery. I had spent most of my childhood in their presence, yet had not even thought about their relationship outside of its intersection with my own. It makes one wonder if great love is a blessing or a curse.

Our people appeared equally distraught over my mother's passing. Slaves almost always act as if they are upset by any ailment to befall their owners, and Winston Jeffers would assert that this was merely a ploy for their own benefit. I however, believed our people's sincerity. It is true that my mother had rarely warmed to them personally, but she also did them no harm. Her kindness was most apparent to Covey and Lizzie and I believe that they conveyed stories of her benevolence to the rest of our people.

A couple of weeks after the funeral, I took another step toward manhood. Just as I had taken the initiative with the slave patrollers, I now thought in necessary to do so with our own slaves. Acting upon my own conscience, one evening I walked out past the grove of maples and pines and rapped on Bartholomew's door.

"Why Massa Gid'in, what bring you out here?" he asked kindly.

"May I come in?"

"Yas, o'course, come on in."

I sat down at the table without invitation. I was not trying to be rude, but was so dedicated in my purpose that I had steeled my nerve and thought about little other than my mission.

"Bartholomew, have a seat please," I said, in an authoritative tone. "Bartholomew, you have been a real asset here at The Copper Beeches. You are the best overseer I have ever seen."

Bartholomew's pride welled up at this compliment, despite the fact that I'd seen very few overseers.

"As you know, I've recently been to Chiltern Grange. Are you aware of how things are run over there?"

He swallowed and sheepishly looked at the ground. He was apparently unaware of where I was going with this and thus unsure how to reply. "Yas sir, I do believes I has a good idea," he replied with a wavering voice.

"Well as you know I will be in charge here one day. And how I run this place depends largely not upon me, but upon you. My uncle needs your help."

At this, Bartholomew diverted his eyes from the floor and cast them directly upon me. I am not sure if it was out of concern for my uncle, or out of relief that I did not profess a desire to be another Winston Jeffers.

"As I said, you are a great overseer. I expect you to not only continue as you have done, but to improve. You will have to assume even more responsibility here. Master Robert needs more rest. He needs less aggravation. He will continue to run things, and I will help him. But you must help us both."

After digesting my comments Bartholomew stood up and extended his hand, which I shook.

"I will do everyting I can."

"Thank you." I turned to walk out, but before I could get out the door, Bartholomew arrested my progress.

"Um, sir?" he stated.

"Yes?" I asked as I turned to face him.

"You not a boy anymore."

I nodded and left. Now, years later I can more clearly understand those critical days in my life. Bartholomew was both right and wrong. I had indeed turned a corner. I was no longer the quiet boy afraid to speak up. Yet I was not a man either. I still had a lot to learn. I think that the best way to sum up my change was that I had determined that fear was useless. Things needed to be done, so I did them. I still preferred solitude to interaction, my books to the fields, and introspection to leadership, but I would no longer shy from any responsibility.

During the period after my mother's death, things gradually stabilized. It's funny how when a major change occurs a new routine emerges, and the new routine becomes the norm. Covey now took a more active role in rearing Eliza and Ellen and I tried my best to keep them on their lessons. Between Covey and myself, we tried to compensate for my mother's absence. We were not wholly successful, given that we each had other duties to attend to as well, but given the circumstances, I do believe that we did a decent job.

Bartholomew was true to his word. He assumed more and more responsibility at the plantation and did an excellent job with each added assignment. I gave him keys to the storehouse and entrusted him with doling out the slaves' provisions. I still kept account of the distribution, but after a while did so merely for record keeping purposes since both Uncle Robert and I had concluded that Bartholomew was completely competent and trustworthy in this new job.

My uncle began to spend more time in his library. He did so with the door closed, and during these times no sound emitted from the room. However, the decanters of whiskey and brandy needed to be refilled more and more often, so there was little secret as to his occupation.

One day Uncle Robert went into Fincastle alone. He said we needed "some things" which I believe meant more liquor. I implored him to take a slave or two with him, but he demurred stating that they were needed in the fields. I do not know at what hour he returned, as I was busy all afternoon tutoring the girls, attending to my own independent studies, and surveying the planting. However, after dinner he called me into his study.

He poured himself a glass of whiskey, and sat behind his desk. I took a seat myself, and was astonished at what he said.

"Your mother made me swear an oath right before she left us and it concerns you." He took a drink from his glass as I sat there dumbstruck at this revelation.

"Your mother was not an... overt person. That is to say she was not always transparent with her feelings. I'm sure you know that she doted on you. She felt that you had no equal. She had

75

no doubt that you would one day do a great job running The Copper Beeches, and was most impressed with your intellectual capacity. She made me swear that if it were at all possible, I would find a way for you to pursue your classical education."

My heart jumped. University? Study abroad? This elation quickly dissipated however, as I returned to the realities that I could not leave my uncle alone. He needed my help too much. As it turned out, as my uncle continued the solution presented itself.

"While in Fincastle today I made a most astounding find. I met a gentleman by the name of Alexander Moeller. Professor Alexander Moeller, to be precise. Professor Moeller has taught at the College of William and Mary and The University of Virginia. He has come to our part of the state to work on some sort of a book or something. I shared an ale with this gentleman while in town, and he has agreed to tutor you once a week."

I was astounded and ecstatic at this opportunity. Of course I would have preferred to attend a university in person, but since that was not feasible, this offered a great alternative. I had enjoyed intellectual discourse with my mother, and since her departure, I had no one. This "professor" however, offered an even better situation. I had surpassed my mother's capacities in many subject areas and this was a chance to learn from another rather than being limited to the information in my stash of books.

"What subject does he teach?" I excitedly asked.

"Um. I can't recall," my uncle stated refilling his glass. "You can ask him yourself tomorrow."

Tomorrow! Wonderful! I couldn't wait. Many, at least in my part of the country, would think me a lunatic for being giddy about learning. However, for me this was a great day.

"Now we'll see how smart you really are," Uncle Robert awkwardly forced the jibe that would have fallen effortlessly from his lips not long before.

CHAPTER 5

The next morning I awoke to the sound of the cock's crow. The pink hue of daylight was barely visible through my window. Though I was not due in Fincastle until nine o'clock, I was anxious to meet my tutor, but a bit nervous as well. Many in Botetourt County had commented on my intellect, but to be considered a genius in our rural locale was not a great feat. Now a man of formal learning, who had taught some of Virginia's finest young minds, would assess me. This fact made me a bit apprehensive. I also hoped this man would not be a sadistic taskmaster. I'd read of brutal teachers who were merciless with their students. These and other thoughts were racing through my mind as I silently ate my breakfast.

After my meal I had time to attend to some of my farm duties. I rode about the plantation making sure the hens and hogs were fed and that Bartholomew was proceeding with the planting. It was unnecessary for me to check up on our overseer, but I was trying to form the habits of a planter. The head of a plantation must take ultimate responsibility to see that the farm runs properly, and if there was any lesson to be learned from my mother's death it was that we never know who will leave us or when. Bartholomew was considerably older than I, so God willing, I would outlive him and thus shouldn't rely on him completely.

The morning passed slowly, but eventually it was time for me to be on my way. I went to the stable and threw a saddlebag onto Ajax. Next I led the horse to the front of the house and tied him to the hitching post while I rushed into my uncle's library to retrieve a few books, paper, writing utensils and an abacus. (I was not sure what lessons we would discuss, so I brought

77

implements of nearly every discipline). I was in such a hurry that I almost didn't notice my uncle sitting behind his desk.

"Gideon..." he called, putting the cork back into the bottle.

"Oh... I'm sorry, I didn't see you Uncle Robert."

"Gideon here is a note." He scribbled quickly on a piece of paper and handed it to me, "If you should require anything while in town give this note to Mr. Drower and he will put it on my account. Do you want me to have someone drive you?" his voice slurred.

"Thank you," I said, taking the note from him, "No I have Ajax saddled up and ready to go. I'll be fine. See you this afternoon."

With that I bounded out the door, mounted up, and trotted off toward Fincastle.

Uncle Robert had informed me that Professor Moeller was staying at Mrs. Evans' boarding house at the entrance to town. I reigned in Ajax outside of the Evans place, and much to my surprise an elderly Negro, perhaps in his sixties, scurried over from across the street and tied up my mount.

"You mus be Massa Gid'in." he said.

"Yes."

"I's Darius. I belongs to Massa Alexander. He inside, go on in. I'll take care o' yo horse."

I removed my saddlebag, ascended the front steps and rang the bell that hung next to the door. In less than a minute I heard the heavy footsteps of Mrs. Evans. Mrs. Evans was a childless widow of about fifty. She was a heavyset, no-nonsense woman that rarely smiled. Beneath her crusty exterior however, lay a good heart. She was brusque and curt, but generous and kind. She did not accept platitudes well and was embarrassed at any recognition of her goodwill. She was an avid cook and would often beckon children to her kitchen window and hand out a piece of pie, cake, or candied apple. Any thank you however was quickly brushed aside as she shooed the child away with his or her treat.

"Hello there, Mr. Gideon," Mrs. Evans stated curtly, wiping her hands on her apron and pursing her lips. "Well, don't just stand there, come on in. The professor is in the parlor. You know where it is. Hurry now!" she said, clapping her hands as she returned to the kitchen.

I entered the room slowly, curiously surveying the bright interior. I found my quarry across the room, in the corner by the window. There sat an elderly man dressed in gentlemanly attire. He was on the thin side, had snow-white hair, and wore a close-cropped moustache and beard. Upon his nose rested a pair of spectacles and he appeared to be reading intently. Despite the commotion caused by the impatient landlady he appeared oblivious to my presence. I stood for half minute in silence. Finally, without looking up from his text, he waved his hand, beckoning me to come closer. As I neared, he pointed to the chair opposite him, still without averting his gaze from the book.

After I had been seated for about ten seconds or so the professor closed the book on his finger and removed his spectacles. He cast his pale green eyes on me and said nothing for another ten seconds. I fidgeted in my chair. Finally he spoke.

"So you're the local prodigy?" he exclaimed with a grin as he nudged my knee with the book.

I was much relieved to discover that he did not appear to be the harsh taskmaster I had feared.

"Um, I suppose," I humbly answered.

"Now, now. After I spoke with your uncle, I made some inquiries around this burg. The general consensus is that you are quite the genius. A bit odd, but very bright," he smiled.

"I have taken a hiatus from my duties at William and Mary to analyze the flora and fauna of this part of our great state. I am working on a study to differentiate the plants of eastern and western Virginia."

"So you are a professor of botany then?" I interrupted.

"Not at all. I have taught many subjects at the university: History, Rhetoric, Philosophy, Literature... but never Botany. My expertise is in the social sciences. However, my interests are quite varied. I grow board easily and when something piques my interest, I have a tendency to pursue it. You see, I was in Richmond several months ago when I came across a most unkempt looking mountain man. He had on his person what he called 'black berries.' He offered me a few and I must say they were delicious. Black berries, as you surely know, are a most ubiquitous fruit. However, I had never tasted flavor of this variety! He confessed that he had brought them from the 'Valley of Virginia.' This occurrence diverted my thinking to the notion that different varieties of the same genus may yet be unclassified within our own state. I therefore asked for a leave from the university to pursue this hypothesis!"

The peculiar exuberance of this old gentleman was quite endearing. He was eccentric, of that there could be little doubt however I liked him immediately. I only hoped that he could offer me the intellectual stimulation I so craved.

"Now listen, young man. I am happy to provide you with some tutelage; however, I cannot allow you to get in the way of my work. Do you understand?"

"Yes, sir."

"Now lets see what you have there," he said grabbing my saddlebag and rifling through the texts I had brought. Mathematics...very good. Okay. Ahh Aristotle. Excellent. Excellent. *The Iliad.* Quite good. What's this? Cooper? *Last of the Mohicans*? Wonderful. We will begin with this."

I was a bit dazed by the professor's whirlwind approach. He jostled me back to attentiveness however.

"Have you read this work, young man?"

"Yes." I replied, a bit confused. You see I had meant to bring a book on the Roman Empire, but had mistakenly grabbed Cooper's novel instead, as their jackets were both the same color.

"Sit yourself at the table over there, and write an exposition comparing the characters of Natty Bummpo and Chingachgook in *The Last of the Mohicans*."

I took the volume from the professor and seated myself at the table across the room. I thought long and hard before I began to write. I had read the book some months earlier, and I had to reflect upon the subject matter. Added to this was the fact that I greatly wanted to impress my tutor. First impressions are important, and this gentleman had already alluded to my alleged "genius." Although he may have been jesting, I felt pressured nonetheless.

While I worked, the professor returned to his book. After about an hour I had finished. I put my pencil down and sat quietly waiting for Professor Moeller to notice. I had not been done two minutes when he beckoned me over again, without averting his gaze from his reading. Again he pointed to the opposite chair and after a brief interlude put down his own text and took up my essay.

He read silently and nodded or shook his head sporadically. In my character analysis, I took the liberty of describing the development of these personages as they moved through the different volumes of *The Leatherstocking Tales* since I had read all five (though of course Chingachgook does not appear in *The Prairie*). By my analysis, in *The Deerslayer* Natty was Chingachgook's protégé. The young white hunter respected his older friend and aspired to be like him. Chingachgook was a young man himself in this work, though he already displayed the characteristics of the stoic, honorable Mohican chief. In the *Last of the Mohicans*, the relationship had shifted. This story was set during the French and Indian War, when white encroachment

81

had increased substantially. I asserted that by this time, Chingachgook and Hawkeye (as Natty was called in this volume) were more or less equals. Hawkeye was the intermediary between and his Indian friend and the British officer Duncan Heyward, but both (and Chingachgook's son Uncas) were instrumental in saving Major Heyward's fiancé and her sister. In *The Pathfinder,* the balance shifted again. With further white settlement (this story was set on the Great Lakes) Natty assumed an even more dominant role. By *The Pioneers* the balance had completely tipped. In this work, the elderly duo are no longer nomadic hunters, but sedentary residents of what would become "Cooperstown." The noble chief had been reduced to a shell of his former self; alcoholic and despondent, eventually meeting his death. The last of the stories, *The Prairie*, has Natty pushed further west by the ever-increasing white settlement, where he eventually dies a very elderly man though the character remains noble; unlike the demise of his Indian friend.

I anxiously awaited the Professor's critique. Finally he put the paper down and removed his spectacles. He took a long breath and then addressed me with those pale green eyes.

"I have both some good and bad things to tell you. First, your analysis is excellent. I could not agree with you more. Cooper's characters definitely follow the path you have described and your thoughts on the subject are insightful, and your writing style is both clear to read and direct. In the negative however you did not follow my directions. I did not ask for these characters to be analyzed throughout their lifespan. It would have been completely acceptable to do so if you had clarified it with me first. Had you told me that you had read all of *The Leatherstocking Tales* and asked if you could expand your study, I would have agreed. However, by forging ahead without getting approval, you gave apples when I asked for oranges." He leaned closer to me. "This is very important, young man. In life, if you do not follow direction it could end in calamity. Now I know this is a small example, but always remember to follow direction, and if you are not sure or do not understand, ask questions before proceeding."

At the time, I extrapolated upon the assignment because I was trying to impress my teacher. However I must admit that I remembered and adhered to this advice not only during my tenure with Professor Moeller, but long afterward as well. It was one of those bits of veiled wisdom whose relevance becomes glaringly apparent at a later time. During this "War Between the States" I have often seen good men die because commanders acted without clearly understanding their orders. Almost as often I have seen young officers try to impress their superiors with their bravado by overreaching. Such actions have usually resulted in equal tragedy. The professor might not have known it at the time, but that innocuous little piece of advice later saved lives of men under my command.

After this lesson, Professor Moeller put down his volume and gazed out the window for a few moments, leaving me to endure the silence. Finally he blurted out, "I would like to inquire about your horse."

I must say, the request caught me off guard. "How do you mean?" I sheepishly returned.

"Hmm. Well is there anything unique about him?"

Frantically searching my mind for some sort of an answer I replied, "He was born a breech and nearly didn't survive."

"Really? Tell me about it."

"Well, he was born on our plantation, but when we realized that there was a problem with the delivery we called on one of Colonel Jeffers' slavess to help. He is the closest thing to an expert in this area…"

"What was the slave's name?" he interrupted.

"His name is Heracles."

"Did he wrap the foal in a blanket after he was born?" he asked, rubbing his beard between his thumb and forefinger.

"Yes." I replied, a bit confused by the question.

He looked back out through the window. "He's a fine looking steed. Is he fearless or is he skittish by nature?"

"He's quite plucky; has been from birth. Even when we tried to hold him down to inspect him, he threw us off and stood on his own."

The Professor digested the information for a few moments and then stated: "I am going to hazard a guess at his name. Is it Ajax?"

I was dumbfounded by the old man's apparent psychic abilities. "H-How did you know that?"

"I am right then?" he laughed. "It was really just a guess. I couldn't be very certain. However, I will tell you why I selected 'Ajax' as my supposition. If you recall, I examined your books upon your arrival. Now you packed several academic volumes, but most telling among your selections were the adventure tales you brought along; *The Last of the Mohicans* and *The Iliad*. Now these selections are not unusual for a bright young boy such as you," he smiled with a twinkle in those green eyes, "but they gave me a bit of a clue."

He nudged my knee with his forefinger before continuing. "Next I listened carefully to your account of the horse's *birth*. Obviously this was of key interest to you, or you would have picked another story to tell. I could not make any connection to any of *The Leatherstocking Tales*, and your admission that a 'Heracles' had saved your horse led me toward the other volume you had packed, *The Iliad*. I scanned my memory for applicable tales from Homer's epic, and I came up with that of Ajax. I surmised that this particular warrior might be the beast's namesake because I guessed that you were familiar with the story where Hercules covered the child Ajax with his Lion's pelt, which was said to have given him invulnerability (except of

84

course for his armpits and neck). Since you are a bright young man and an avid reader of the classics, I felt that you would see your horse's birth as analogous to the Greek hero Ajax."

I was aghast at his deductive powers. Of course he erred in thinking that I had named the horse, when it had actually been my mother, but the professor had outlined her thought process completely. My tutor obviously read the amazed look on my face.

"Now, now, young Gideon," he laughed nudging my knee with his book "it is not magic, and to be honest, I was quite lucky. You presented a few clues and I took an educated guess. I could have very likely been wrong, in which case the expression on your face would not be one of awe, but of confusion and disappointment."

Nonetheless, I was impressed with his powers. He went on to explain that such lines of reasoning are by no means assured, especially when dealing with morons. He explained that since I was a "thinker" he had increased his odds at the outset. Fools abound, and employ little rhyme or reason for the decisions they make where the intelligent individual is more likely to apply logic and rationale to their choices.

The Professor stared out the window again, in a meditative state, and then suddenly asked me if I owned any books on political thought. I searched my memory, visualizing the rows of books in my uncle's study. The fact that I had to scour my mind indicates the lack of experience I had with the material.

"I believe that I have some works by Thomas Paine and also Edmund Burke and I'm sure that we have a copy of Thomas Jefferson's *Notes on the State of Virginia*. There may be others, but I cannot be certain."

"Well I would like to explore this subject matter on your next visit. Please read as much as possible in the area of political philosophy. Read whatever you have available: Burke, Paine, Jefferson...etc. and we will share some thoughts next week."

85

With that I bid farewell to my new mentor. I crossed the street to where his man had hitched Ajax and I trotted home reflecting on the professor. I recollect that his eccentricity caused me to break into a chuckle, though my thoughts were quickly sobered as I pondered the lessons. He was odd, that was certain, but probably brilliant as well. His knowledge base was quite extensive, and he not only possessed a great deal of information but was able to make use of it as well. I remember my mother once told me that "the value of knowledge was not in its possession, but in its use." I had harbored a small degree of concern that Professor Moeller may be a virtual encyclopedia of facts, yet not be able to demonstrate practical application of his ideas. When this occurs, the learner often wonders *why* he is asked to commit effort to such study.

During the next week, I was forced to spend a lot of time in the fields. Summer had broken and our people were hard at work cultivating the corn crop. Weeds were rapidly overtaking the rows and Bartholomew was driving the teams hard in order to remove the invaders. Some could be hacked away with hoes, but this was tricky as the hand wielding the hoe had to be very skilled so as not to damage the corn stalk. Due to this, most weeds had to be extracted by hand. As our people worked at pulling the weeds, another problem emerged: root rot.

Most of our corn crop was "sweet corn" which is very susceptible to root rot. Bartholomew explained that the most effective prevention of this affliction is planting the corn in a field that was previously used for soybeans. However, we grow very few soybeans, so we could not delegate our corn crop to only that small parcel of land.

Our cornfield sloped toward the south at approximately a thirty-degree angle. It was at the southern most area of the field that Bartholomew discovered the disease. The rot is caused by excess moisture in the soil, and presumably, since water flows downhill, the corn in the lowest area was most affected due to inadequate drainage.

Bartholomew showed me the telltale signs of the blight: the leaves had dry tips and were turning yellow. Fortunately we caught it early, and our driver's extensive agricultural experience provided a solution. First, we had to sow potash into the soil in order to increase its fertility. Next, in order to keep the soil drier, we had to aerate it. Our people had their hands full trying to save the afflicted corn while maintaining the crop that was not affected. Uncle Robert was made aware of the situation, and did come out to survey the field, but he dedicated little effort to managing the operation. This was basically left in my hands, and I in turn gave Bartholomew free reign. However, I had to oversee Bartholomew, since I had to absorb as much of Bartholomew's knowledge as possible if I wanted to become a successful planter.

The problem with the corn impeded my reading assignment, however I did my best. I was able to read in the fields between interruptions. Though this was not as fruitful as I would have liked, I continued my studies in bed, forcing poor Covey to maintain her sentry duty over my bedside candle.

Among our books I found Thomas Paine's two pamphlets that had been so influential during the American Revolution, *Common Sense* and *The Crisis*. We had a copy of Burke's *Reflections on the Revolution in France*. I also located some work by Jean-Jacques Rousseau and John Locke's *Treatises of Government*.

I became immersed in the political ideas of these individuals. It was interesting to me that so much of what I read was already part of common thought in America. I held or had heard discussed many of these ideals without knowing their specific origin. Indeed, most of the adults of our community seemed to believe that most of these ideas originated with Thomas Jefferson. Perhaps this was an effort to further canonize one of

87

Virginia's favorite sons, or maybe it was due to pure ignorance. Regardless, as usual my curiosity piqued at the exposure to this new intellectual stimuli.

The week rolled past and though I had read and constructed notes on a great deal of material, I still felt inadequately prepared for my meeting with the professor. As a result, I decided to write a letter of explanation requesting more time, and have one of our people take it into Fincastle. None of our workers could be spared from the fields, but after the workday was completed I secured Uncle Robert's permission to send Jacob into town. Jacob would have to go without dinner in order to deliver the message, because it is illegal for slaves to travel at night. I could have indicated on the pass that Jacob had permission to travel past dark, but I did not trust the patrollers to honor such an excuse.

Therefore, I had Jacob saddle a reliable horse and make haste for town. I felt bad about forcing him to miss dinner, so I slipped him two pieces of silver for his trouble.

Since the onset of my uncle's depression I had to devote more time to the fields, which meant that I could no longer tutor my cousins after lunch. Therefore I moved their lessons to after dinner. I was juggling my duties at The Copper Beeches, my own studies and teaching the girls, and regrettably their learning suffered. I was not able to work with them as much as I would have liked, though they did not mind so much since they were not extremely interested in intellectual development. We were going over some simple mathematics when I heard a horse trotting up the drive. With a glance out the window I confirmed that it was Jacob returning.

After stabling his horse, Jacob entered the house through the kitchen. I left the girls in the study and went to find out what the professor had said.

"Well Jacob, did the professor give you a note for me?"

"No sir…"

"Did he give you a message?" I anxiously broke in.

"No sir..."

My heart was palpitating with the fear that my request had offended my tutor. "Well what happened?" I barked.

Had he been a white man, Jacob may have retorted, "If you'd shut up I'd be able to tell you!" But of course such a thought never crossed his mind.

"De man wasn't home. I left yo letter wit Misses Evans."

"Oh. Alright. Thank you, Jacob. Here..." I said handing him a plate of leftovers I had Covey make up after dinner.

"Tank you Massa. Dees fine vittles."

"Bring the plate back tomorrow."

"Okay, I will Massa."

With that he scurried out the back door. I finished working with the girls and then returned to my own studies, hopeful that the professor would not be angry.

Just as we were finishing breakfast the next morning, Cicero knocked on the kitchen door.

"Come in!" Uncle Robert bellowed, sounding much like his former self (of course it was early and he hadn't hit the bottle yet today).

The old Negro shuffled in followed by Darius, the professor's servant. Uncle Robert scratched his chin for a moment and then recollected who our visitor was.

"You're the professor's boy, right?"

"Yas sir." he replied, with eyes cast downward. "I comes wit a message fo young Massa."

He reached into his pocket and handed me a note.

It read:

> Dear Gideon,
> I understand your dilemma.
> Presently I am quite preoccupied
> with my own project. Come next
> week at the scheduled time.

Respectfully,

A. Moeller.

I bid Covey to retrieve a pen, ink and paper from the study and I hastily scribbled a reply thanking the professor for his understanding and affirming that I would most certainly be there at the appointed time.

That week I frantically pursued my studies in between managing the farm and working with my cousins. By the time I was due to return to the professor I felt adequately prepared, but I was still nervous. I hoped my knowledge was sufficient for his purposes.

I filled my saddlebag with my books and notes and rode Ajax into town. I handed my mount over to Darius at the foot of Mrs. Evans' door, flinging my saddlebag over my shoulder. I rapped upon the front door, and heard the professor bellow from inside the parlor.

"Come in, Gideon!"

I entered the room to see two-dozen large books laying in a row on the floor, the professor asserting pressure on the last in line with the palms of his hands. I suppose he read the quizzical look on my face as he chuckled before offering an explanation.

"I am pressing the samples I collected in the field so that I may catalog them."

"Oh." I said, my curiosity relieved.

"Well come over to the chair and have a seat," the professor invited.

Once I was seated, he stared out the window for a few moments and then turned back to me and nudged my knee with his hand asking, "So what did you discover in your reading?"

I found this question infuriatingly vague. "Um, how do you mean?"

"Well, I see that you have Burke's *Reflections on the Revolution in France* as well as Jefferson's *Notes on the State of Virginia*. Though Jefferson's book was written before the French Revolution, he completely supported the Revolution while Burke was in opposition. Whose vision of republican government do you find more compelling?"

I thought for a moment before replying. "Hmm. I certainly concur that their ideas on France are in great contrast, but I found it interesting that the differences seem to have roots deeper than is readily apparent. In all honesty Professor, I knew very little about Edmund Burke, so I first explored some biographical material. It appears that Burke did not consider himself a political philosopher, but a *political writer*. He was very distrustful of abstract thought and thus tried to apply ideas to practical, concrete subject matter. Jefferson however, was a devotee of the enlightenment thinkers and thus preoccupied himself with philosophy and the application of ideals in the abstract."

The professor was clearly impressed with this analysis, as his pale green eyes were transfixed upon me. "Yes. Yes. Completely true. But how do you apply this to their opinions regarding republican government?"

"Well," I began a bit more confident, "despite their differences on the French Revolution, the two were not in completely different camps. Burke supported the emancipation of America and of course Thomas Jefferson played an integral part in that movement. Obviously Burke was not a royalist. However, Burke was characteristically pragmatic where Jefferson was caught up in social philosophy. Therefore, I believe that Burke saw events in France from a much clearer perspective than Jefferson. Burke supported republican government, but thought the French Revolution was more an exercise in anarchy than republicanism. He recognized the resultant chaos and the cancerous mob mentality that had formed and despised the consequent disorder and blood bath."

I continued, "Jefferson however was a champion of individual rights and liberal republicanism. His ideals were formulated through digestion of enlightenment thought. Thus when the French toppled the monarchy in 1789, Jefferson saw it as a fruition of the ideas of his heroes, the enlightenment thinkers."

"Interesting…" the professor said. "However, Jefferson did not confine himself entirely to the theoretical. He was one of the architects of American Democracy and thus may have had a stake in the French Revolution. How do you suppose this is true?"

I thought for a moment. "If Jefferson truly believed that republican government was the highest form, the end of Louis XVI's rule in France would corroborate his own role in the American Revolution and the construction of the democratic system in this country."

"Yes. You see Jefferson is strongly revered here in Virginia, so criticism is very limited. You have characterized Burke as a pragmatist and Jefferson as an idealist, but Jefferson had a pragmatic side as well. However much he propagated himself as a social philosopher, he was also a politician and when need be, a pragmatist. For example, are you familiar with Jefferson's opinions on the Bank of the United States?"

A bit embarrassed, I had to admit that I was not.

"President Washington's Secretary of the Treasury, Alexander Hamilton believed that a National Bank was needed. Jefferson, at the time the Secretary of State, opposed this because he was against the Federal Government obtaining too much power. To push his case he employed a *strict* interpretation of the Constitution citing that that document did not expressly state that the Federal Government had the power to establish such a bank. Hamilton countered with a *loose* interpretation stating that

92

the Constitution gave the Federal Government the power to employ any means required for the government to function. Well as I'm sure you are aware, Hamilton's opinions won out. However this is not the end of my tale..." he said, with a twinkle in his eye. "What was the greatest accomplishment of Jefferson's presidency?" he asked.

"The Louisiana Purchase," I confidently replied.

"Absolutely!" my tutor responded, prodding my knee. "Though nowhere in the Constitution does it state that a president may make land acquisitions! What does this tell you?"

"That Jefferson's philosophy was set aside if it conflicted with his practical necessities?"

"That appears to have been the case."

I was astonished at this revelation. In Virginia, Jefferson was an icon.

It appears that Professor Moeller read the disappointment upon my face. "Dear boy, I am not implying that our beloved Jefferson was not a great man, only that he *was* a man, and thus subject to human actions. This is not necessarily a bad thing. Had Jefferson held to his strict construction argument, our nation would be decidedly smaller."

He continued, "Have you ever heard this quote? *The tree of liberty must be refreshed from time to time with the blood of patriots and tyrants. It is a natural manure.*"

"Yes," I replied. "That is one of Jefferson's most famous."

"How do you feel it applies to Jefferson's stance on the French Revolution?" he asked, rubbing his beard with his fingers.

"Mr. Jefferson quite obviously felt that rebellion is a natural, indeed a beneficial occurrence for society."

"Quite!" he replied. "In theory." He smiled devilishly. "Are you familiar with Shays Rebellion?" he asked.

"Not wholly," I sheepishly returned.

"After Independence was gained, the Massachusetts legislature tried to pay off its war debts by raising taxes. Unfortunately many farmers were unable to meet the demand and marched on the capital to prevent the legislature from meeting. The rebellion collapsed when the state militia intervened, but many saw the event as a need for a stronger national government. Jefferson, however thought that the revolt had been justified. He restated his opinion on rebellion urging that Shays and his men be pardoned."

The professor went on, "The reason I mention this is that I want to relate it to another event. Are you familiar with the treason trial of Aaron Burr?" he asked.

I felt a bit of relief, as I was somewhat acquainted with this topic and attempted to relate the events as I knew them.

"If I recall correctly, Burr was Jefferson's Vice President and already in a bit of a bind over killing Alexander Hamilton in a duel. I recollect that he was involved in a scheme to separate the western part of the United States and set himself up as a potentate. The plan failed and President Jefferson had him tried for treason, but he was acquitted."

"Excellent!" my tutor responded with a twinkle in those emerald eyes. "Jefferson was most adamant about seeing Burr convicted and did his utmost to bring this to fruition. Chief Justice John Marshall did not allow this to occur, despite being a kinsman of the president. Why do you suppose Jefferson advocated rebellion in France and in Massachusetts, but attacked Burr so vehemently?"

"I know that Jefferson and Burr were political rivals and Jefferson had only narrowly beaten Burr in the presidential election of '04."

"Quite true. Burr was only denied the Presidency when Hamilton threw his support behind Jefferson. However, refer back to our discussion on self-interest," he said with a nudge.

I scratched my head. "Burr's actions, if true, would negatively impact Jefferson's Presidency, where the other two corroborated his philosophical opinions on republicanism."

"Excellent!" the professor exclaimed. "Let us explore this from one last perspective. Are you aware of Mr. Jefferson's opinions on slavery?" he queried.

"Yes. I know that he did not approve of the institution," I replied.

"Well, that depends..." he replied with a smirk. "Mr. Jefferson certainly stated his opposition in principle. He proposed a clause in the Declaration of Independence abolishing slavery, but quickly abandoned it. He later expressed his desire to see the institution banned in western regions in *Government for the Western Territory*, and still later suggested gradual emancipation in Virginia. However, Mr. Jefferson owned over a hundred slaves and did not emancipate any during his lifetime and only five upon his death. What does this say of his dedication to his principles?"

I thought this a bit redundant, as it quite obviously was another illustration of the same point. "As Burke suggested, abstract concepts are not always applicable to reality," I said.

"In Jefferson's case, this is particularly true in economic terms. Let me read you a couple of items I came across when I was helping a colleague evaluate the economic impact of slavery on Virginia agriculture." He went over to the corner of the room and dug through a stack of books and papers, returning with a faded notebook.

He paged through until he settled on a particular passage. "Mr. Jefferson once wrote 'I consider a slave woman who gives birth to a child every two years as more profitable than the best man on the farm... What she produces is an addition to the capital.' He also wrote to his brother-in-law Francis Epps: 'Nor would I willingly sell my slaves as long as there remains any prospect of paying my debt with their labors.'"

95

I was a bit aghast that the professor appeared to have such strong feelings about slavery. This sentiment prompted me to make a bold move. I stated bluntly, "Sir, you own a slave yourself..." I caught myself mid sentence and bashfully averted my gaze, ashamed of my disrespect.

However, the professor did not take offense. He smiled, and with a flash of emerald from his eye replied, "My dear boy. I am neither defending nor condemning the institution. You are confused as to our topic. Our discussion was on the abstract philosophy of Jefferson versus the more pragmatic opinions of Burke. However..." he continued with a wink. "We have stumbled into an interesting topic. You cannot be unaware of the recent tumult in Congress over the passage of the 'Compromise of 1850.' Our nation is once again polarized on the issue of the expansion of slavery. I think it would be quite fruitful for us to mimic what our statesmen are doing in our capital. We shall analyze the pros and cons of our esteemed institution. I am going to send for literature on the topic. Then, we will each take a side, research it and debate the merits of each. How does that sound?" he enthusiastically closed, poking my knee again.

As I rode home that day, I reverted to my habit of rethinking the lesson. I had to admit that I was intrigued at delving into an issue of such immediate relevance. It would be interesting to participate in a debate on a topic that had so recently been fodder for our country's most revered politicians.

CHAPTER 6

The following Sunday I was emerging from church with the girls (Uncle Robert rarely attended any more) when I saw Darius standing patiently by our carriage. I asked Mrs. Wilson, a fellow congregate, to watch my cousins for a few minutes, and as the pair scampered about with the other little girls, I strode over to my tutor's boy.

"Hello Darius, are you waiting for me?" I asked the old fellow.

"Yas sir. Massa Alexander sent me ta fetch ya. He over on yonder porch," he replied, motioning with the hat in his hand toward Mrs. Evans' place.

I took a moment to confer with our slaves, telling them not to tarry too long in town. I likewise gave my assent for Ulysses to accompany his wife back to Deep Dene for the day and gave him the pass I had prepared beforehand. By this time he was traveling between the two plantations unescorted. Ulysses had proven himself both a hard worker and trustworthy member of our family, and as a reward was allowed to spend as many of his off hours with Penny as was practicable.

I hurried over to the boarding house to find the professor swaying comfortably in a rocker immersed in the Good Book. As was his custom, he finished the passage before addressing me.

"Ah, Mr. Gideon. It's nice to see you on such a pleasant Sabbath. I simply cannot prevent myself from reading, so I figured that scripture was the best fodder for a Sunday!"

I did not know if the professor attended church or not, but religious he must have been; given his choice of reading material.

"Come inside for a moment if you please," he said, rising from his chair.

Following the gentleman inside, he led me to a table filled with a dozen books.

"Our materials have arrived!" he proudly exclaimed, passing his hand over the stacks.   "Now our task is to construct arguments for and against the institution of human bondage. I have no real expertise in the art of debate, so this will be as much of an exercise for me as it is for you!" he laughed, poking my arm. "Hmm. It seems we have a bit of a problem regarding who will prosecute and who will defend," he contemplated, scratching his chin. "We are both Southern gentlemen, and both are in possession of Negroes." He tapped his forefinger on his lips and then abruptly continued. "Have you a coin, my boy?"

I was initially taken off guard by the request, but recovered to produce a piece of silver from my pocket. "It seems that the only equitable way to solve our dilemma is by a toss of the coin," my mentor stated as he examined the currency.

I had been so preoccupied with my duties at The Copper Beeches during the interceding week, that it had not occurred to me that I might have to support abolition! The thought horrified me, and I listened with trepidation as Professor Moeller continued.

"If the head side comes up you will defend our peculiar institution. If it is the tail side, I shall defend it. That seems fair does it not?" he asked, with a chuckle.

In actuality I did not think it fair at all. It was not I who invented this exercise! When a gentleman is challenged to a duel, he is at least afforded the opportunity to choose his weapon. However, he was the teacher and I the student, so my objections went unvoiced.

I could feel a bead of sweat trail down my temple as my tutor tossed the piece into the air. The coin tumbled upward, held momentarily at its apex, and then made its descent in the

98

same fashion, coming to rest on top of the stack of papers on the table.

"Tails," I said, with audible dejection.

The professor apparently did not perceive my dismay, as he bundled up the material I would need to digest. He called for Darius, who brought in a small trunk. Into this luggage he stacked several books as well as some loose papers and notebooks. Next he turned to me with a warning.

"Now Gideon, I would advise you to keep the contents of this trunk, and the nature of our exercise, a secret. Fincastle seems to me to be semi-moderate in temperament, but they are by-and-large an uneducated lot and would fail to perceive the intellectual value of our enterprise. They would probably evaluate the material in that trunk as mere propaganda and not look too favorably upon you. We will meet back here in two weeks at the regular time in order to conduct our debate."

The professor made this statement with a smile and a gentle poke on my arm. I believe that in his eccentricity he failed to understand the degree of danger involved in possessing abolitionist literature. At the time, the situation was not as hazardous as it would be in two short years when *Uncle Tom's Cabin* was published. It will be remembered that that work ignited a conflagration of abolitionism in the North and a subsequent vehement reaction in the South from which I could never have escaped. Yet, even in 1850 it was illegal to possess such books. Given my status in the community it is unlikely that I would face a lynch mob if my assignment were found out, but I definitely would have been cast in an unsavory light that would have made my life quite difficult.

After my meeting with the professor I collected my cousins and drove home. On the ride I pondered the assignment. I had mixed feelings about the project. I was certainly not anxious to adopt the Yankee side of the argument. I was a Virginian and an aspiring country gentleman. Many Northerners misunderstood us; they simply did not understand our culture. They did not seem to see that their attack was not on slavery, but our entire way of life, Negroes included. The Black population was not separate from our world, but an integral part of it. On the other hand the assignment had provided me with not only an opportunity to explore the genre of rhetoric and debate, but also presented a great challenge. To defend one's own opinions is much easier than to defend those of an opponent. As I pulled into the drive of The Copper Beeches, I had concluded that all in all this would be a worthwhile exercise.

In between my other duties at the farm I dove into my research with ardor. I kept the trunk locked in my bedchamber, and I procured a leather satchel to transport documents to and from the fields during the day. I never appreciated Bartholomew's abilities more than during the time I was preparing for my "debate." In theory I was supervising the slaves, but if one were to observe my activities, I would have been found with my nose buried in a book, pamphlet or newspaper, intermittently scribbling in a notebook. I was safe in this practice among our slaves, as they were illiterate, but I was sure to keep a lookout for Uncle Robert. If he were to sally up, an involved explanation would be required to justify the materials in my possession.

My resources involved several volumes of abolitionist literature as well as dozens of copies of newspapers such as William Lloyd Garrison's *The Liberator*, and Frederick Douglass's *The North Star*.

Always the logical thinker, I concluded that the most efficient way to organize my case was by dividing the abolitionist argument into three areas: religious, moral, and legal. In my examination of the material, I found that all opposition to our "peculiar institution" could be classified under one of the aforementioned categories.

In arranging my presentation of the religious argument against slavery I of course had to add the "Good Book" to my source material. As a devout Christian I was certainly already familiar with the Bible. However I now had to put the scriptures to pragmatic use. The abolitionists made frequent use of the Bible in their cause and for credibility's sake I now had to corroborate any references they made to God's word. As I pursued this endeavor I began to see the Bible in a different light. I rapidly became aware of the fact that it is a very equivocal book. It became readily apparent that one can use biblical references to prove or disprove almost anything. Southerners had always used it to justify slavery and yet it was also the main weapon of the abolitionists.

Most of the literature I encountered did not impress me. Most seemed silly, dubious propaganda. Due to my assignment I made use of such items, but it had little impact upon my personal opinions. This however changed one night about one o'clock in the morning.

I was in my bedroom but had vacated my bed in exchange for the floor. I found that it was easier to work from the varied and numerous documents by spreading them out before me. I was lying on my stomach, a pillow under my chest examining numerous items by candlelight when I began to read a volume I had not yet explored. The book had been published by the American Anti-Slavery Society, so I had put off its examination, as I surmised that it was probably strict propaganda. It was entitled *American Slavery As It Is: Testimony of A Thousand Witnesses*. This work was eleven years old and had been complied by Reverend Theodore Dwight and sisters Angelina and Sarah Grimke. I say "compiled" because the book was an assemblage of first hand accounts of slave abuse.

Key to the abolitionist argument was the contention that the slaves were grossly mistreated. I have often been privy to adults discussing this concept. In our own locale, the abolitionists'

101

cries of abuse were met with both anger and laughter. Most regarded the anti-slavery element as being full of "hogwash." They were regarded as outsiders who pontificated from their northerly regions using abstraction and conjecture. It was commonly held that such individuals had never been to the South and thus did not have a leg to stand on.

As I began perusing the book I was taken by the apparent credibility of the "witnesses." The authors took pains to provide the specifics of each subject including which states, counties, and even individual plantations they had visited and even the duration of their stay. Affidavits and oaths were also provided to attest to the witnesses' character. I'm sure that some Southerners would quickly dismiss such items without really exploring them, but given the nature of my assignment I did not discard these sources so quickly.

The stories presented by the aforementioned witnesses were quite riveting. Some were brutal accounts of outright abuse, while others described more subtle forms of maltreatment, but most were believable and consequently, unsettling.

A Mr. Caulkins described the events he witnessed on a North Carolina plantation. While there, he observed an overseer receive payment from the plantation owner (more than once) via the use of a negress in lieu of money. She was provided for him to exercise his personal pleasure (the eventual result being a tribe of mulatto children). In another incident, Caulkins tells of a slave trying to flee when accused of stealing a hog, only to be shot by the overseer. The slave survived the blast of birdshot, but carried pellets under his skin long after the incident. On the same plantation Mr. Caulkins witnessed the overseer's wife order a slave to sell a hog at market. She did this without her husband's permission and when he became enraged, she said the slave had stolen the pig. The slave was "terribly" flogged despite the fact that the plantation owner said that he believed the slave's story. He simply refused to dishonor the white woman by calling her a liar.

Mr. Caulkins also told of some particularly brutal events involving a runaway. The runaway was captured, shot, and decapitated. His head was then carried home for the other slaves to see. Another runaway was placed in a hole in the ground and buried up to his neck. He was left in this state for five days.

On a neighboring plantation, the witness described a negress who would not submit to her owner's advances. He had her flogged, and said he intended to continue to do so every day until she complied with his wishes. She eventually "gave herself up to be the victim of his brutal lusts."

Another of the witnesses was the Reverend Horace Moulton, who spent five years in Georgia. Many of his observations were benign, discussing slave housing, food, clothing, etc. Much of this Mr. Moulton found to be an abomination, but his arguments were less than convincing. However, when he began to describe slave punishment his contentions become more compelling. He describes some brutal floggings (much more brutal than the one I witnessed at Chiltern Grange). He explained that often slaves' punishment did not end with the flogging. "Sometimes after being whipped, some have been shut up in a dark place and deprived of food, in order to increase their torments. I have heard of some who have, under such circumstances died of their wounds and starvation."

The Reverend described other torments as well. He stated that many women miscarried due to being whipped. He described seeing slaves whose backs and shoulders were complete scar tissue as a result of the lash. He stated, "Children were whipped unmercifully for the smallest offences, and right before their mothers." He also recounted other physical abuse aside from whipping. Heads laid open with clubs or canes, jaws broken, teeth knocked out (or in), ears slashed off, hot irons used

103

to brand slaves for identification... The horrific accounts went on and on.

Miss Sarah Grimke herself provided some testimony as her father was the late Judge Grimke of the Superior Court of North Carolina. Miss Grimke's account is particularly credible as she is herself a Southerner who "deserted the home of my fathers to escape the sound of the lash and shrieks of tortured victims..." This witness described a slave forced to wear a "choke collar" which consisted of a leather strap fastened around his neck and tethered to one ankle. If he strode too far, he would cut off his airflow, and strangulate. She also described a woman who slit the ears of her maid for some trivial offense. Most disturbing was her description of a runaway slave's severed head displayed atop a pike along the roadside.

The tortures described were not confined to physical abuse. Miss Grimke told of a cruel (and one might even say blasphemous) game played on a slave. She recounted a tale of a master and his dinner companion debating whether Christian slaves were sincere in their religious professions. The master said that he owned a slave who would rather die than renounce Christ, but his friend did not believe him. The owner sent for the poor soul and ordered him to deny his belief in the Lord Jesus Christ. The slave pleaded to be excused and continually affirmed that he would rather be killed than deny the Redeemer. The master became enraged that the slave refused to obey his order (this is insane since the slave was proving his master's contention) and had him severely whipped. During the flogging he continued to refuse to blaspheme, so the whipping continued; eventually resulting in the man's death.

I stayed up late into the night reading the aforementioned and other accounts contained in *American Slavery As It Is: Testimony of A Thousand Witnesses*. I must say the book certainly contained its share of dubious stories and trivial accounts. As a whole its message was not entirely compelling.

However, some of the specific testimonials were from believable witnesses and thus quite credible. What most struck me was not really the tales themselves, but the realization that they were *plausible*. As stated earlier, most people (myself included) develop their sensibilities from personal experience. In our part of Virginia slaves were not in abundance, and those that did exist were generally treated quite well. I had thus assumed from my own observations that slavery in Botetourt County was a representation of slavery throughout the South. Now, I realized the folly of this shortsightedness.

I began to extrapolate upon the aforementioned notion by pondering how it would be possible to assure that slaves were treated humanely. I found this idea to be analogous to a maze without an exit. Even if state (or God forbid Federal!) legislation were to be enacted to protect the slaves, it would be unenforceable since slaves were kept on private residences, obscured from public view. Additionally, slaves were property, and the Constitution protects citizens from governmental interference in property rights. I was troubled by these ideas, not only because of their moral implications, but because in my three pronged approach to attacking slavery (moral, religious, and legal) I would have to use legal justification to "prove" it unlawful.

Luckily, I found a volume among my materials that could aid me in my legal argument. In the days that followed I tore through *Illegality of Slavery* by Benjamin Shaw.

On Sunday I impatiently sat through our church service, as I knew that I would have the entire day to devote toward my assignment. Uncle Robert made it to church that day but the service tarried on the steps engaged in some menial conversation with Mr. McBride. As I anxiously waited to drive home I wondered if my uncle's companion could smell the brandy on his breath. Finally, we collected the girls and climbed into the buggy. I assumed the reins as Uncle Robert swayed in the seat

105

beside me. Waiting under the tall pine was Ulysses, his hat in his hands. Ulysses had proven himself, as he had said he would, and was allowed to travel to the Janus place on Saturday afternoons and spend the night (provided he accompanied Penny to church on Sunday). After church they would remain together either at the Janus plantation or our own. As we approached, I speculated whether he would request to go to Deep Dene, or if he would ask if his wife could accompany him back to our plantation. I wagered on The Copper Beeches. Our carriage halted alongside Ulysses so that he might speak with Uncle Robert.

"Does Massa mine if Penny comes back fo' de day?" he sheepishly asked.

My uncle looked over his shoulder to make sure that none of Fincastle's White residents were within view, and then quickly removed a flask from his inside pocket and hammered down a quick swig.

"No. That's fine." The humor had all but left the once sly soul. He took another hasty gulp and motioned me onward without a word.

That Sunday was a bright, warm day. My mother would have called it "glorious." I was anxious to get to work, but I simply could not stay cooped up in my room on such a day. I loaded my materials in a saddle bag, grabbed some biscuits and ham from the kitchen and trotted off on Ajax.

After hitching Ajax to a bush, I laid a blanket out on the ground under a large poplar tree and spread out my books, papers and notebooks. There was a pleasant breeze blowing from the west that wafted the scent of lilac from a nearby tree. As agreeable as this zephyr was, it made it difficult to work. I gathered some flat stones from the along the creek and strategically used them to keep the volumes open to the appropriate pages and to prevent the newsprint from blowing away.

106

I worked happily for two hours before breaking for lunch. Though the meal was a simplistic one, it has stuck in my mind as one of the best I have ever taken. I clearly recall lying on my back staring up at the poplar leaves blowing in the breeze as the brook gurgled melodiously and the lilac perfumed the air. In the short interims when the wind died off, I could hear the faint song and laughter from the village beyond the grove of maples and pines.

The afternoon was so relaxing, and I had been pushing myself so vigorously, that I actually drifted off to sleep. I awoke with a start as the page of a book began to waver violently from a strong gust that had tossed the paper weight carelessly aside. The sky was murky and Ajax pawed at the ground and neighed alarmingly. For a moment I thought night had fallen, but then a large drop of rain plopped upon the text in front of me, then another and another. To my astonishment, the bright blue sky had dimmed into a leaden gray. I quickly regained my senses and in a whirlwind collected all of my materials, thrust them into the saddle bag and vaulted aboard Ajax.

As I hurried home the rain began to come down in sheets. The sky was painted charcoal gray, though clouds of a lighter hue swirled beneath the blacked out sky. Thunder began to crack loudly at my heels; so close by that it was deafening. It grew difficult to see as I sped through the gathering puddles and ensnaring mud.

I began to worry if I had lost my way, when suddenly I saw the stable illuminated by a blast of lightning. The latch had come undone from the large double doors and one was swinging violently in the maelstrom. With God given luck I timed the opening perfectly and galloped through the orifice.

I was out of the tempest, but did not feel safe yet. I was soaked to the bone, and desperately desired to change clothes and warm by the hearth in the parlor. Thus I quickly tore the saddle and bridle from Ajax, thrust him into a stall and burst out of the barn at full speed, stopping only to lock the doors behind me.

"Lordy Massa! We been plenty worried 'bout you!" Covey exclaimed as I exploded in the kitchen door.

Uncle Robert came staggering in from the study, bottle in hand. His look of alarm quickly dissipated into a half smile as he surveyed my drenched condition. He opened his mouth to utter what I'm sure was meant to be a witty remark, but he became confused and said nothing.

"I'm going up to my room to get changed!" I half yelled as I bounded up the back stairs not wanting to waste the time to travel around to the broad staircase reserved for the White folk.

The storm was one of the most violent to ever hit the valley. The rain came down in sheets, followed by hail, and then more rain. The wind sounded like a locomotive as it barreled over the farm. The thunder boomed like a cannonade and rattled plates in the cupboard. Most thunderstorms, especially the severe ones, are relatively brief, but this one lasted through the night. The lightning that cracked around the house was so bright that in the sudden moments of illumination I could see all the way to the storehouse.

Uncle Robert tried to ignore the storm and was reading some forgotten volume in between gulps of brandy. My cousins and Lizzie stayed close to Covey who was trying her best to prepare some food in the kitchen. I however was fascinated by the tempest and moved about the house peering from various windows, curious as to what might be seen from each. By the time I fell asleep, the tempest was still blowing.

The next morning my uncle awakened me just before dawn. He ordered me to get some breakfast and survey the plantation for damage. At the breakfast table, Uncle Robert nonchalantly explained that any damage to our buildings was of much less consequence than that done to our crops. The buildings could be repaired, but the crops could not be replanted this season. I recall that I was amazed at his casual manner over this very substantial point. It was becoming apparent that my uncle was slowly drifting toward total apathy.

I exited the kitchen door and shuffled down the back steps, only to find my progress impeded by Ulysses and Penny. I had completely forgotten that Penny had been at The Copper Beeches.

"Massa, I's couldn't git Penelope home las' night." He said with eyes downcast. "I's berry sorry. Dat storm came up so fast and den it got dark, but de storm kept up anyways..." The poor fellow stammered out his apology obviously frightened that I would be angry, and possibly with the foresight that I might not permit her to ever visit again if the skies looked overcast.

"I certainly don't think you're to blame. You don't control the weather do you?"

"Umm. No..." the confused Negro replied to the rhetorical question.

"You did the right thing. You came to me at first light, and you can take her home now. I'm sure Mr. Janus will understand what occurred. Go down to the stable and hitch up the wagon, then take her home. I will write you a pass and tell Bartholomew where you are when I ride the plantation this morning to survey the damage."

Oddly, the usually obedient slave did not scurry off to the stable. "Massa... I's can't take her back by mysef. If'n I does, Massa Janus goin' to whip Penelope."

"What? No. He is a reasonable man. He will understand. Off you go now."

Yet the slave stood his ground. "Sir, I doesn't tink you knows dis man. He don't even want to let her come to de Copper Beeches. It only because he afraid of Massa Robert dat he give in. Please Massa. I begs you to come wit us an esplain it to him." He knelt before me after he said this, dragging his wife to her knees as well.

I was moved by this humble plea and even though I was certain that he was wrong about Henry Janus, his sincerity and conviction made it impossible for me to simply dismiss his request. Ulysses had proved himself to be a faithful, hardworking, and trustworthy member of our "family." Even though Winston Jeffers had endeavored to convince me that darkies were tricky by nature and could never be trusted, I could not see any possible way Ulysses could benefit by being deceitful. If what he was saying were untrue, there would be no need to involve me at all. My first inclination was to give Ulysses a note of explanation to present to Janus, but I remembered the impracticality of this plan since Penny's master was as illiterate as she.

"Okay. Get up. Get up," I said, feeling uncomfortable at their genuflection. "Go to the stable and hitch up the wagon. Penny you run back to the village and tell Bartholomew what we're doing. Tell him to survey the storm damage, and I will be back directly."

"Tank you! Tank you Massa!" Ulysses was so relieved at my decision that he tried to kiss my hand. I yanked my hand from his grip, both appalled and embarrassed by this act of devotion. As the couple scampered off to their tasks I re-entered the house to inform my uncle of the situation. He was completely disinterested however, and bid me to do whatever I liked as long as I inspected the damage upon my return.

I walked out to the stable to find Ulysses finishing his task. However, something in the barn caught my eye.

"You all hitched up Massa!" Ulysses yelled, interrupting my thought.

"Fine. Go report to Bartholomew, and make sure Penny hurries back here," I replied, sliding past him into the stable.

"Yas sir!" the slave answered back as he sped off.

What arrested had my attention was my saddlebag. In my haste the day before, I had neglected to bring my materials back

110

into the house. I had become so consumed by the storm that I had completely forgotten my resources. I hurried over to reclaim my prize but something looked askew. To this day I can't quite explain what piqued my suspicion, but something did not seem quite right. Admittedly I had been in such a hurry that I had no recollection as to the manner in which I had left it. Yet... My speculation was interrupted by the arrival of Penelope. I quickly gathered up the saddlebag and tossed it into the back of the wagon. My cargo and I boarded and we were off to Deep Dene.

As we made the trip to the Janus place, evidence of the storm was everywhere. Tree limbs were strewn about and great puddles had pooled in low-lying areas. About halfway to Deep Dene, we encountered an oak that had been uprooted and was blocking the road. Luckily a coil of rope was lying in the wagon bed. I was forced to unhitch the horses and laboriously drag the tree from the road.

An hour had passed by the time we traversed the little structure that bridged the dene. As we crossed, the noise of violently rushing water sounded beneath the span. Looking down I could see that the storm runoff was forcefully chugging through the dam. Casting my eyes downstream I could make out the figure of Henry Janus at the second dam. He was directing his two male slaves who were arduously attempting to open the duct at the spillway to allow for the increased flow of water. It is doubtful that he could hear our approach over the din of the cascade, yet somehow he was immediately aware of our presence. I could see him bark out some directions to his people before hurrying toward us in as close to a run as his rickety legs could muster.

We pulled up in front of the house, and Penelope climbed out and stood a step behind me, eyes downcast in deference. Though she spoke not a word, I surmised that she was frightened. Janus thumped up all out of breath. He removed his hat, wiped his brow with a rag, and settled his lungs before attempting to speak.

"I was worried sick about you, girl!" he thundered to Penny. "Go on and get to the back of the house, the Misses is trying to board up a busted window." With that the little polka dotted kerchief bounded off.

"I was goin' to ride off to see your uncle at first light, but the vent is stuck on the dam. If'n I don't get it open, that pond will flood the crops; hell even my house will be under water!"

I could see that Mr. Janus was frazzled by his dam malfunction but I could also detect a strong current of anger as he scowled after the retreating negress. Though it was apparent that he wanted to get back to the dam, I thought it prudent to probe old Henry.

"Did you think that we had stolen Penny?" I asked with a half-smirk reminiscent of my uncle at an earlier time.

"No. No, of course not," the anxious man replied, dabbing his brow again.

"I apologize for not sending her home last night, but if I had, it is quite likely she would have been killed."

I got the feeling that Mr. Janus was definitely irritated that Penny had not been returned Sunday evening, but he realized how foolish he would have looked trying to combat my logic.

"Umm. Well I thought she would be back earlier this morning," he said, laboring to cover himself.

"Well sir, I left at first light. I suppose that I could have been a few minutes earlier, but we were delayed by an oak that had fallen across the road."

I observed Mr. Janus's body language during this exchange. He nervously rocked from one foot to the other. He fidgeted with his hat, and he was sweating inordinately. Finally he blurted out, "Of course it ain't *your* fault. That girl has got to be more responsible, that's all there is to it!"

It became apparent to me that Ulysses' concerns were warranted. I wasn't convinced that Janus would go so far as to whip Penelope, but I certainly got the impression that she was in for some rough treatment. He might even bar her from coming to The Copper Beeches. Since Ulysses had obviously been correct in assessing Janus' temperament, I thought that perhaps he was also correct in gauging the man's trepidation of my uncle. Since I had become my uncle proxy in virtually every other capacity, I decided to speak for him now as well.

"Mr. Janus. You know my uncle thinks highly of you..." At this he perked up. His reaction was of near surprise, but he was obviously pleased by my untruth. "Just yesterday he said how clever it was of you to allow Penny to continue to visit her husband at our place. He said that it was obvious that you knew that making your slaves happy was the easiest way to ensure that they work their hardest for you."

Janus seemed a bit confused, but nodded in agreement. Quickly, he caught on and smiled broadly at being given credit for such a grand idea.

"Uncle Robert told me that he would be very displeased if Penny were to express any displeasure to Ulysses. He is a good worker and if she were unhappy, it would make him unhappy. If he is unhappy he will be of less use to us."

The simple man was too stupid to know he was being manipulated, but was bright enough to catch the veiled meaning. I could read the mixed emotions on his face. He was proud of the perceived esteem he held with my uncle, but less than thrilled with the restraint that had just been put upon his control of his own slave.

Yells from the lower dam startled the befuddled fellow as he quickly bid me farewell and hurried back under a labored gait.

I returned to The Copper Beeches and quickly unhitched the wagon. I was anxious to comply with Uncle Robert's directive, so I saddled Ajax and tossed the saddlebags on his back. I rode

113

round the barn, past the springhouse and bee house and then down to the storehouse. Surprisingly, there was almost no perceivable damage to these structures. Of course some downed tree limbs littered the grounds, but I was shocked at our good fortune regarding our out-buildings. I turned to head out to the fields, but held for a moment. My view drifted past the grove of maples and pines and suddenly I decided to first head to the village.

The village was deserted of course since all of our people were out in the fields. Unfortunately the flimsy cabins had not held up as well as our more sound buildings. The damage was fairly extensive. I left the village rather quickly. Seeing the state of the slave quarters I became alarmed over our crops, which of course were even more delicate than the nigger shacks.

I found our people in the south pasture. The men were repairing a fence, and the women were applying braces to some damaged trees in the apple orchard. As I approached, Bartholomew hailed me.

"Let's have it, how do things look?" I asked the driver, trying to mask my apprehension.

"Well sir, you ain't gonna believe it..."

I gulped awaiting the bad news.

"...but dis is de worst of it, right here. It plain amazin' but de crops was all but spared. I tinks de Good Lord was on our side!"

I was speechless for a moment. "You mean the wind, the hail... it didn't cause any damage?"

"Not really, sir. Oh we had some water collect in de low ground. Had to bail out some'o de corn, but some how we lucked out! Afer' we done dis we can get back to work cultivatin'."

I paused for a moment, astonished at our good fortune. "No." I said authoritatively, which caused Bartholomew to register an expression of shock. "I was just at the village. After

114

you're done here I want you to go to take a wagon to the storehouse and get whatever lumber and tools you need to repair your homes. Spend the rest of the day taking care of your cabins."

The overseer smiled. "Tank you Massa. Dat right kind 'o you. I knows dis is a busy time fo' de farmin' but we did git hit right hard las' night. I was hopin' you might let us off early to start fixin' de cabins, but now I knows we won't be sleepin' under de stars tonight!"

During this exchange Ulysses, who was mending the fence not ten feet from me, kept glancing nervously in my direction. After I was done with Bartholomew, I rode off a few yards and beckoned Ulysses to follow. He sprinted over to my side and removed his hat, looking up anxiously.

"I had a little talk with Mr. Janus. I explained to him that my uncle would be very displeased if anything were to happen to Penelope. He caught my meaning. I believe that everything will be fine."

"Oh tank you Massa. Tank you. I knowed you'd do de right ting."

I was struck by Ulysses' devotion to his wife and his gratitude toward me. I was in such a benevolent mood that a thought suddenly crossed my mind. "I know that you have been selling some of the vegetables from your garden plot in town. Maybe one day you'll have enough saved to buy Penelope's freedom."

At that moment it did not register how ridiculous my suggestion actually had been. By the time Ulysses had enough money to buy his wife he would be a hundred and fifty years old. Plus, he would first have to purchase his own freedom, which in itself was not a possibility.

"Dat man never sell her!" I was taken aback by the brutal contortion of Ulysses' face as he blurted out his anger. His demeanor had always been polite, deferential, and affable, but

115

his features contorted into a grotesque expression of vehemence. He quickly caught himself however and shook off his irritation. His usual pleasant countenance returned and he thanked me again and rushed back to work on the fence.

CHAPTER 7

I ate a hearty dinner and settled into bed in order to ensure that I was well prepared for the debate upon the morrow. Unfortunately, my rest was interrupted about four in the morning by an unbelievable front of wind that blew in from the west. At first I thought the storm had returned, but as I gained my senses and peered out the window I ascertained that it was wind and wind only. It was quite an inexplicable event. I remember talk of a twister once touching down in the valley years ago, but this was no twister. This wind was very much like that which usually accompanies some sort of moisture; be it rain, hail or snow, however the massive gusts were dry as bone. The odd event lasted about an hour, and then all was quiet again.

I rode into Fincastle ready to intellectually spar with an opponent who was obviously out of my class. Of course my task was even more impossible given the fact that I did not even support the cause I was forced to defend. At first my predicament made me frantic. However, I was able to resolve the conflict by equating myself with an attorney who must defend a client he does not like. Given the circumstances, I was unusually confident.

I was shown into the boarding house, but before I could enter the parlor, Mrs. Evans thrust a piece of pie into my hand. I was not hungry, but I thought better of refusing. Though the portly woman acted hard-as-nails I knew that she delighted in doling out her baked goods and any rejection would have hurt her greatly.

I thanked the landlady as she thumped back toward the kitchen and staggered my way into the parlor, plate in hand and saddlebags over my shoulder. The professor was seated in his customary spot in the corner by the window, book in hand as usual. I was struck by the odd title of his reading material: *Tales of the Grotesque and Arabesque.*

My mentor finished his passage before addressing me. "Ahh, I see Mrs. Evans got you two!" I noticed the remains of his own slice of pie on the table next to his chair. "Well have a seat at the table, my boy!" he boomed, gesturing toward the work area.

The professor had obviously already prepared himself. At one side of the table were several meticulously organized folders. Next to these was a blank tablet and pencil. He placed both of our slices of pie on the surface and poured a glass of cider for each of us. He motioned me to occupy the position across the table.

I sat down and arranged my own documents in a similar fashion. Professor Moeller seated himself and patiently waited for me to finish.

"Shall we begin our little discussion?" he asked, with a flash of those green eyes.

I glanced apprehensively at the door. My trepidation did not go unnoticed by my mentor, and he yelled for Darius. The old Negro appeared out of nowhere.

"Darius, kindly close the doors will you?"

"Yas Massa."

"Does that make you feel better?" the old man laughed to himself, sensing my relief. I certainly did not want any fragments of my argument leaking out into Fincastle. "Would you like to begin, or should I?" he continued.

I was nervous, but also anxious. I indicated that I would like to start the discussion. I began by reading from a prepared introduction, as a lawyer would an opening statement.

"The topic of emancipation is both controversial and volatile. I have endeavored to present the argument for the abolition of slavery by providing three grounds for

118

emancipation: Legal, Religious, and Moral. First I would like to present the Legal component of my argument."

The professor interrupted me. "Fine. Present your first element. Then I will present my rebuttal. Then I will present one of my points, and you will be given the opportunity to rebut. We will alternate in this fashion until we have concluded.

"Ahhem." I cleared my throat in preparation. "Yes. First let me begin with the origination of slavery on this continent. Our current chattel are the ancestors of those brought here, since the importation of slaves was banned in 1808. The original slaves were forcibly taken from their homes in Africa and removed across the Atlantic against their will. This is by definition *kidnapping*. Kidnapping is illegal in this country, as in the British Empire (of which we were a part before the War for Independence). Therefore the importation of slaves was illegal from its inception."

Content that I scored heavily with my first contention, I continued my legal argument. "Our legal system prescribes, through habeas corpus, that individuals cannot be indefinitely detained without due process of law, meaning a trial by a jury of their peers. Slaves are held without *any* trial, let alone one by their peers (which would require other slaves as jurors.)"

The professor had begun to scribble some notes as I asserted my points. This unsettled me a bit, but I proceeded nonetheless. "The Declaration of Independence states that ...*all men are created equal, and are endowed by their creator with certain unalienable rights; among these are life, liberty, and the pursuit of happiness.* Clearly, slavery violates these precepts. Slaves do not have their liberty, and this being so, are also denied the right to 'pursue happiness.'"

I consulted my notes for a moment and continued. "Americans are guaranteed rights under local, state, and federal statutes. Among these levels of government the federal is of course the most predominant. This was established by the adoption of the Constitution. During the Constitutional Convention, Southerners were distressed over the amount of power northern states would accrue in the legislature due to their superiority in population. The result was 'The Three-Fifths Compromise' which established that slaves were to be considered *three-fifths* of a person when apportioning taxes, and representation in the legislature. Therefore the national government established, and the state governments agreed, that slaves were three-fifths of a person, yet they are granted *no* rights. By the aforementioned bargain, slaves should at least have three rights for every five granted to whites."

I continued, "Finally I direct your attention again to the Constitution; the highest law of the land. This document's first ten amendments are called 'The Bill of Rights' yet nowhere in this list is it stated that people have the right to own slaves, nor does it mention anywhere in its entirety that states have the right to protect slavery. What it does state is that every state in the Union must guarantee a *republican* form of government. A republican government means *representative*. Slavery compromises this in two ways. First, slaves are denied the right to vote, therefore an enormous proportion of the population is denied participation, and thus true republican government does not exist. Secondly, there are no Negroes in public office; therefore the current government (local, state and federal) is likewise not truly representative."

I closed my folder and folded my hands atop it. I tried to act confident and composed as I yielded to my opponent across the table. The professor finished jotting down a few words and then looked up at me smiling.

"A fine job I must say. However, I of course have the duty of opposing your stance. Let me see…" He rearranged his notes and folders before beginning his rebuttal. "Your first point is an interesting one. You contend that the original slaves were kidnapped. I will not dispute this. I will concede that it is fact.

It is indeed foolhardy to assume that anyone volunteered for a life of servitude. However, I assert that the abduction of a man from the Guinea coast in 1690 has little bearing on the situation in the United States of 1850. A statute of limitation exists on all crimes but murder. Therefore, a crime that was committed generations ago cannot be punished in the present. If a man stole his neighbor's chicken a hundred years ago, his great-grandson cannot be held accountable for his ancestor's misdeeds, nor can he be made to relinquish the eggs produced by that chicken's ancestors. Likewise, the perpetrator, (in this case kidnapper) cannot be brought to justice because he is long since dead. There is no precedent for depriving people today of property acquired, though possibly illegally, generations ago."

"Next you addressed the notion of illegal detention. You are of course correct when you assert that our legal code prohibits individuals from being held without due process of law or the suspension of habeas corpus. *However* there is a flaw in your argument. These principles apply only to citizens, and as you are well aware, slaves are not citizens."

I had not overlooked this point, but rather I had attempted to phrase my argument in such a way as to disguise this flaw. In retrospect I can see that it was a sophomoric attempt at best. Unfortunately I was well aware that once my opponent exposed this weakness he would be able to hammer at it again and again.

"Your citation of the Declaration of Independence is one that has been made by many others arguing your case. Yet the citizenship precept applies here as well. Mr. Jefferson cites that "life, liberty, and the pursuit of happiness" are rights endowed by God. If they are guaranteed by the government, as you contend, then non-citizens (slaves) are not protected. If they are granted by God, then God gives them to whom he sees fit, and since Blacks do not have this right, *He* obviously does not deem them worthy. I will not digress too far into this line of thought

121

however; as I know you intend to address the religious reasons for abolition."

He paused briefly before continuing. "In your citation of the Constitution you explore the absence in the Bill of Rights of a declaration that citizens have the right to own slaves. This is because the Constitution guarantees the right to own *property*, and as you know, slaves are property. It would be illogical for our founders to enumerate each and every article of property that an individual is allowed to own. For example, the document does not specifically state that a man has the right to own a cow, yet this is not contested. Also, the Constitution states that the states assume powers not specifically enumerated as 'Federal.' Therefore the absence of any discussion of slavery only increases the claim that States have the right to allow servitude."

"You also cite the 'Three-Fifths Compromise' as part of your 'Constitutional argument.' You are correct that the compromise provided that a slave constitutes three-fifths of a man, but not all men are citizens and thus not all men are guaranteed rights. You also contend that the Constitution requires republican government. This is true, but voting rights are determined by the states. Some require written tests, some require the ownership of property, and all require that the individual be male. So, voting rights are not granted to everyone *except* the Negro. Women do not vote, nor do they hold office, yet they are represented under our system."

I knew that my legal argument stood on shaky ground; especially since our system of law is founded upon English Common Law which itself is based on *legal precedent*. This of course means that it is determined by previous court rulings. Since our courts have never ruled *against* slavery or *for* the rights of Negroes, the legal facet of my argument had the narrowest base of my three avenues of attack. I tried to keep my emotions in check even though I was quite dejected by my mentor's deconstruction of my argument.

The professor rearranged his material again, and then began to present his first point. "I am impressed with the organization of your position." He reached into the corner and grabbed his walking stick and quickly prodded my arm across the table to emphasize his affirmation. "I believe that I will take up your second point as my first. This way we can kill two birds with one stone." Evidently, Professor Moeller intended to present religious evidence in defense of slavery.

"I have seen you each and every Sunday, come into town to attend church services. Therefore it is obvious that you are a devoted Christian. As you are aware, the Bible has two major divisions, the Old and New Testaments. I first draw your attention to the second book of the Old Testament. In the Exodus, God declared that the Hebrews were his "chosen people." These "chosen people" had been enslaved by the Egyptians and through God's grace were led out of bondage by Moses. Now, some have contended that the Hebrews' deliverance from slavery indicates that the Almighty does not approve of the practice of slavery..."

I had been formulating just this thought for a rebuttal, and was jotting down this point when I caught the familiar emerald flicker from my opponents gaze as he again prodded my arm with his cane.

"...However, this notion must be quickly dispelled. Why is this? Because the Old Testament is pregnant with accounts of the Hebrews themselves owning slaves! Therefore, God does not oppose slavery itself, only the slavery of certain peoples. If the Almighty wanted the Negroes free, he would free them, as he did the Hebrews."

I quickly scribbled a few thoughts in my notebook, as I believed that I had found a small chink in this notion. However, my exploration of this thought would have to wait until my rebuttal.

The professor continued, "Since we are on the Old Testament, I shall present another piece of evidence from that particular section of the Good Book. I am sure that you are familiar with the story of Noah. It will be recalled that Noah cursed his son Ham, and through extrapolation, Ham's son Caanan." He opened a Bible to a marked page, adorned his spectacles, and read: "*Cursed be Caanan; a slave of slaves shall he be to his brothers.*" He continued, "Not only is this direct evidence that God supports the idea of slavery, but that he condemned Ham's tribe to servitude *ad infinitum*. We well know that the Hametic people are the Negroes."

Professor Moeller took a sip of cider before continuing. "Since we are Christians, let us now look to the New Testament. During the thirty-three years our Savior spent on Earth he preached about many, many practices that he deemed sinful. The list is too long to enumerate in our short time together," he chuckled, again tapping my arm with his stick. "Yet, Jesus never condemned slavery. Peculiar is it not? The Son of God, sent to us on a divine mission to save us from eternal damnation did not even address the issue of slavery. Slavery existed at the time. Jesus waded through slaves in the streets of Jerusalem. However, nowhere in his teachings do we find condemnation of slavery. Why is this? Well the conclusion is elementary: God does not oppose slavery."

The professor went on, "I do not wish to go into too much Biblical detail so as to avoid belaboring the point. However, I do have two final bits of religious evidence to present. It is well known that it is the duty of every Christian to convert heathens and therefore save their souls. Africans are not Christians. Missionaries had attempted to convert them to Christianity through peaceable means, but their efforts have almost always ended in disaster. Though it may seem harsh to have forcibly transplanted these heathens to this continent, their time spent here is but a moment when compared to eternity. If they can be successfully converted to Christianity (as most slaves have been) they will reap the benefits of paradise in the hereafter. Therefore the institution of slavery is actually beneficial to them in the long run."

I jotted down a few more notes as I was confident that I had identified another hole in the professor's argument.

"Finally," he concluded, "God supports slavery. How do we know this? The clearest evidence is its very existence. It is often said that 'God works in mysterious ways.' I am not sure why the Almighty approves of slavery, but he obviously does. If he did not, it would not exist." With that he closed his folder and patiently awaited my rebuttal.

Most abolitionists were devout Christians, so my research had produced considerable ammunition for the religious argument. However, the format of our debate suggested that I must confront my opponent's assertions. Perhaps I could finagle additional information into my counter-argument, but this would have to be done tactfully, to preserve the integrity of the prescribed format.

When the professor began to discuss the enslavement of the Hebrews by the Pharaoh, I was prepared to leap all over this point. The fact that God ordered Moses to lead the Israelites *out of bondage* provided me with a potent arrow for my quiver. My hopes were quickly dashed however, when the professor exposed that the Hebrews themselves held slaves. I was forced to try my hand at the "chink" I believed I had found.

"It is true that God had Moses deliver his people from Pharaoh's grasp," I began, "but the Hebrews were not liberated overnight. They were held in bondage for generations before they gained their freedom. Since God allowed the Hebrews to remain slaves for some time, and then provided for their eventual freedom, the same may be true of his plan for the Negroes. Indeed we may be on the cusp of the time that God has appointed for their release, and just as Yahweh sent Moses to

125

free his people, God may have also sent the abolitionists to do the same for the Negroes."

At the time I had no idea how prophetic this notion was to be. It was nine years later that that zealot John Brown tried to seize the federal arsenal at Harper's Ferry and arm the slaves. Ironically he claimed that he was acting on God's orders.

The professor sat silent through my response, respectful of the format that had been established. He smiled slightly as I began my next rebuttal.

"I am familiar with the story of Noah's son and grandson. However, there are sufficient examples from the Old Testament that contradict any sanctioning of slavery." I shuffled through my notes searching for such evidence. "Exodus 21:16 states: *He that stealeth a man, and selleth him, or if he be found in his hand he shall surely be put to death.* Jeremiah 22:13 provides another example: *Woe unto him that buildeth his house by unrighteousness, and his chambers by wrong; that useth his neighbors service without wages and giveth him not for his work.*" I knew that my examples were a bit ambiguous, but I was also content that they were no more so than the examples my adversary had cited.

"You discussed the fact that Jesus did not condemn slavery. Perhaps he did not do so directly, but his teachings lead us in that direction. The Lord said to 'love thy neighbor.' He likewise treated all with equal respect, even harlots and lepers. Also, Jesus' disciples carried on his teachings, and they confronted slavery more directly. In James 5:4..." Consulting more of my notes I stated: "...it says: *Behold the hire of the laborers who have reaped down your fields, which you kept back by fraud, crieth; and the cries of them who have reaped are entered into the ears of the Lord of the Sabbath.* Also, Timothy 1:9-10 states: *The law is not made for a righteous man, but for the lawless and disobedient, for the ungodly and for sinners, for unholy and profane, for murderers of fathers and murderers of mothers, for*

126

*manslayers, for whoremongers, for them that defile themselves with mankind, for **menstealers**, for liars, for perjured persons. "*

I thought for a moment, as I took a drink of cider. The professor remained respectfully silent, giving me his undivided attention.

I continued, "You mentioned that it is the duty of Christians to convert non-believers, and that slavery helps accomplish this. I am not so certain. First, slaves know that most masters want them to believe in Christ. Acting as Christians gets them privileges, or at the very least prevents much punishment. Thus many may espouse Christianity without really believing. It is certainly in their best interest to do so. I have heard of accounts where masters have found odd arrangements of chicken bones and idols in slave cabins, even in the homes of slaves who had made the most ardent display of their Christianity. This is evidence that some continue to practice heathen ways despite their master's influence. Therefore, a slave's perceived devotion to the Lord may be a farce."

Next I presented my conclusion. "Sir, you contend that the very existence of slavery proves that God supports it. This however is far from certain. Murder, adultery, idolatry all exist but it is doubtful that God approves of them since he prohibited them in the Ten Commandments. There is much evil in the world, and it is not logical to suggest that God approves of evil deeds."

I concluded in what had become the customary fashion of closing my notebook and folding my hands atop it. My instructor smiled broadly from across the table.

"Well done. Well done. I believe it is your turn to present. Moral reasoning? Isn't that your next point?" He returned to his attentive demeanor, prepared to listen to my third argument. I recall that the professor's conduct both amused and soothed me. I was certain that he would take offense at my efforts to attack his ideas. It is only natural for one to do so. However this was hardly the case. He seemed to revel in each point I scored.

My third avenue was the most compelling, and the most often used weapon of the abolitionists. Slavery tugged at the conscience and thus opponents often assaulted the morality of anyone who owned slaves. I rearranged my papers to produce one that contained my prepared text on the subject. I briefly scanned the material and then deviated slightly so as to include some of the content already covered in the debate. Admittedly, much of what I was about to say was material paraphrased from noted abolitionists such as Garrison, Douglas, and Beecher.

"You have contended that anyone who is not a recognized citizen of this country is not protected by its laws. We have differed over whether slavery is supported by the law of God and man. However there is yet another area that transcends the minutia of legal jargon and the ambiguities of the Bible. This is the simple truth of morality. Slaves are not citizens, but they are most definitely *people*. Some people in this country are considered property. But should they be considered as such? Many assert that the answer is 'no.' The most fundamental rule taught to children is 'to treat others as you would like to be treated yourself.' How many of us would assent to being treated as the Negroes are treated? I have not read of one instance where a white person has volunteered to do so."

"Aside from the so-called 'Golden Rule' is the fact that many slaves are mistreated. In my possession, I have a volume that relates incidents of rape, mutilation, murder and kidnapping." (I described the break up and sale of slave families as 'kidnapping' for lack of a better term). "I will not subject you to the multitude of examples that litter the aforementioned text, as I am sure that you are not unfamiliar with such accounts since you provided the very volume of which I speak. It was established earlier that slaves have no rights. This being the case, individual acts of abuse cannot be prosecuted. Property

128

rights are protected, and thus a master may do what he wants with his slaves. Therefore, the only recourse for ensuring the moral treatment of all *people* is to abolish slavery!" I briefly lost my composure and banged the table with the flat of my hand upon concluding my argument.

I had become so impassioned in the presentation of this last point that I momentarily forgot that I was not espousing my own beliefs, but regurgitating the views of noted abolitionists. As I quickly recovered from my intoxication I'm sure my facial expression betrayed my embarrassment. However, Professor Moeller merely smiled and gave me a wink.

"Ahh, a difficult point to contest! But I will try nonetheless. Morality. Would it be moral to turn an infant out into a snowstorm? Certainly not! Yet emancipation would do just that. Scientific evidence shows that Negroes, or more accurately the *Negroid race* are inferior to White men. The data on this topic is too voluminous to list, so I will confine it to a general fact: No item of social, practical, scientific, or other value has ever been found among the sub-Saharan African cultures. This truth has followed the Negroes across the Atlantic. They possess the mentality of children. The great majority of masters are not their tormentors, but rather their protectors. They provide food and shelter to this God-forsaken lot. If left to their own devices, these poor souls would surely perish. Therefore it would be *immoral to free them.*"

The professor removed his spectacles and rubbed the bridge of his nose, momentarily giving the appearance of a weary man. Upon replacing them however, his vigor returned.

"You have cited the fact that some masters commit acts of cruelty. This cannot be denied. However, I have already stated that *most* masters are *not* cruel. This being the case, the whole system should not be brought down due to the abuses of a small minority. Some people mistreat their dogs. Should dog ownership then be banned? Of course not."

129

"Finally I must address your last sentence whereby you *insist* on emancipation." He smirked and nudged my arm with the walking stick as I sheepishly looked away. "If these millions of illiterate, unskilled, childlike, 'people' were let loose... what then? How would they survive? They know but one thing and that is farming. Where would they get land to farm? Do you suppose that Whites would voluntarily relinquish acres to the Negroes? If not, would the government force them to do so? Remember, constitutionally, citizens are protected from seizure of their property. Would the Negroes move north and take factory jobs? How do you suppose the Irish and other immigrants who populate the cities would feel about that? Freeing the slaves would not only be detrimental to the Black man, but the country as a whole."

We both sat silent for a moment. My mind was spinning with the equally compelling, yet completely conflicting, fodder of our discussion.

"Well what do you think of our little exercise?" the professor finally asked with a grin.

I did not really know how to answer. I scoured my brain for an accurate adjective. In desperation I settled for the oblique "Enlightening."

"I must say you performed wonderfully, Gideon. It is a difficult question is it not?" he chuckled to himself. "Unless I am gravely mistaken, it is unlikely that those boys in Washington City will be able to untangle this knot!"

A knot. Yes. That was an appropriate analogy. Unfortunately, it did not appear that anyone was trying to untie it. Rather, it looked as if the knot had both ends exposed, and each side was tugging at their respective end with all of their might. The result of course was to make the knot tighter and tighter. Occasionally the sides would take a break and set the knot aside for a while, but it could not be ignored, and this tug-of-war would always reconvene.

130

"How do you like the enterprise of debate?" he asked.

I had to answer honestly. "I do not care for it very much."

"Ha!" he laughed, slapping his knee. "Why is this?"

"Well, I did not mind the research aspect, but I really don't care for the confrontational nature of the debate itself."

"I see..." he said, scratching his beard. "You know Gideon, if you are to run a plantation you must be able to assert yourself with White men as well as Black. It is easy to command slaves, they are used to it. They put up little resistance, and even if they do, you have the power to punish them. However as a businessman you will have to deal with a bevy of suppliers, brokers, transporters... etcetera. They will be looking out for their own interests, not yours and you will often have to confront them to ensure your needs are met."

I appreciated the professor's effort to apply the exercise to what he was sure would be my life-long occupation. He was certainly correct. However he did not foresee my future as a military officer where these skills would be of even more benefit. Not only did I have to command my men, but I often have had to argue my position to superiors.

"You, my boy," he said, pointing at me with the cane, "had the more difficult job. We are both Virginians, and as such are both familiar with slavery and the arguments for it. I would wager a guess that the information I gave you was the only abolitionist propaganda that you had ever seen! Yet the flip of the coin dictated that you oppose slavery. I must say young man, that you rose to the occasion. It is difficult enough to organize and elucidate an argument for a debate, let alone one that you have little knowledge of, or belief in."

My instructor kept his attention focused on the exercise itself. He did not return to the details discussed during our discussion. This omission intrigued me. I wondered if the sly smile and twinkling green eyes indicated that my mentor meant to educate me beyond the mere art of debate. I remember the

131

professor's words blurring before me as I tried to peer past the objectivity of the academic rhetoric and ascertain Professor Moeller's true feelings on slavery. Unfortunately I did not possess the ability to dispel the fog surrounding my tutor's personal feelings or expose any hidden agenda. If he had indeed endeavored to alter my own perception on the subject, he had succeeded. I did not have any great epiphany. I did not suddenly convert to the doctrines of abolitionism. However, I found myself inadvertently thinking about the subject often. The complexity of the matter vexed me. As a boy bent on solving problems, I was frustrated by the fact that this issue appeared to be an inescapable conundrum.

The professor and I were enjoying another slice of Mrs. Evans' pie when we heard a commotion outside. Looking out the window we saw a young man galloping down the street. I recognized the unusually large head of Winston Jeffers. He was yelling something, but I could not make out what he was saying. Putting aside our pie, the professor and I walked out to the front porch. We were quickly joined by Mrs. Evans who had stomped her way out from the kitchen.

"What in tarnation is going on?" the landlady angrily barked, as she continued to dry the dish in her hand.

"It appears that this young man is a bit agitated," the professor responded lightheartedly.

I waved my hand above my head and after a moment, Winston recognized me. He sped toward us from the other end of the street.

"Winston. What in God's name is the trouble?" I asked, confusedly.

"Gideon! Janus is dead!" he spat out.

CHAPTER 8

"What?" I replied, shocked. "How? What happened?"

"I don't know much. I was on my way into town when I was overtaken by one of Janus's slaves. He said his master had drowned and that Mrs. Janus was frantic and had sent him into town to bring aid. Since I was on my way to Fincastle anyway, I sent his boy back to Deep Dene and told him to assure his mistress that I would roust the undertaker. However, Jervis is not at his shop. Do you know where he is?"

"I'm sure you can find Mr. Jervis at Drower's," the landlady interjected. A typical busybody, she apparently was aware that the undertaker was at the general store.

"Thank you, ma'am." Winston replied, with a tip of his cap. "I've got to go, Gideon. I'll talk to you later." With that he galloped off.

I was still dumbstruck by the revelation. It was a long moment before I regained my senses. Mrs. Evans hurried off down the street to confer with the other hens of the town and surprisingly the professor was also excited. His natural exuberance was about to boil over.

"Darius!" the old man yelled at the top of his lungs. The servant quickly materialized out of nowhere. "Darius, hitch up the coach." Then turning to me, the professor asked, "Do you know the way to this *Deep Dene*?"

"Why yes. Janus is our neighbor," I answered, perplexed by his actions.

"Wonderful! Will you accompany us?"

"To Deep Dene?"

"Of course!"

I nodded in the affirmative, still unsure what was going on.

"Umm. Professor... Do you think we should stow our debate materials before embarking?" I asked, fearful someone would stumble upon the abolitionist literature.

"Right you are my boy. Right you are," he chuckled, taking me by the arm.

We quickly collected the documents and deposited them in a large trunk (after relocating some of the professor's botanical samples). Professor Moeller also packed a leather bag for the trip. He threw a half-dozen items into the satchel, but I was only able to identify one. Curiously, he had included the book he had been reading upon my arrival.

We emerged from the house to find that Darius had followed his orders accordingly and the buggy was ready and waiting.

"Your plantation is near that of this Mr. Janus?" the professor queried.

"Yes," I replied.

"In that case, why don't I have Darius hitch Ajax to the carriage. We can ride there together and then you will not have to travel all the way back here before returning home."

I readily agreed and climbed in place beside my tutor. Darius tied the reigns of my mount as instructed, and then assumed his position as driver. In a moment we were trotting toward Deep Dene.

I liked the professor and had become more comfortable in his presence, however I still deferred to his status and age. I was simply bursting to know why he was so anxious to reach the Janus place, but respect and natural timidity prevented me from inquiring. I'm sure that Professor Moeller sensed my curiosity, and I believe that he was attempting to play coy with me for his own amusement. However, he was unsuccessful in containing his effervescent nature.

He burst out, "Between my botanical jaunts I have been reading an exciting collection. Have you ever read anything

134

from this author?" He pulled the aforementioned volume from his bag and handed it to me.

I examined the author's name: Edgar Allan Poe. I thought for a minute as I looked through the table of contents. "I think I may have read a poem or two in a magazine, but that was a few years ago. Didn't he pass away sometime last year?"

"Indeed and under most curious circumstances. He was found delirious in a Baltimore gutter, and died a few days later without recovering his senses." He took the volume from my hand and pulling a small pencil from his breast pocket circled a number of stories listed in the table of contents. "Take the book home with you. I want you to read the selections I have listed," he directed, handing the book back to me.

As we bounced along, I opened the front cover of *Tales of the Grotesque and Arabesque*. The book was not very thick. It contained twelve "short stories." The professor had circled four in particular: *The Gold Bug, The Murders in the Rue Morgue, The Mystery of Marie Roget*, and *The Purloined Letter*.

I had heard of the author, but I was not much for contemporary literature. Poe in particular did not lend himself to my situation. He had published his stories mainly in journals and magazines few of which ever made their way as far west as rural Botetourt County. I was more acclimated to reading classic volumes that could be procured and added to one's library. Apparently (according to the publishing notes) the edition now in my hand was a compilation, a reprinting of some of Poe's most famous tales.

The professor interrupted my examination by chucking, "Do you recall the day I guessed your horse's name?"

"Yes," I replied, replaying the incident in my head.

"I think you will soon see where I obtained my method!" he said tapping the book with the copper head of his walking stick.

Before long we were rattling across the causeway over the Deep Dene. Darius pulled up in front of the meager house and we were immediately met by Gus, the eldest of Janus's three slaves. I recon the old fellow was about sixty or so. His son Cy (also one of Janus' slaves) was only about twenty years younger.

"Oh Massa Gid'in it you? I taught it be Mr. Jervis."

"Where is the corpse?" my mentor broke in.

"De what?" the ignorant old fellow responded.

"The body, boy, the body," The professor impatiently exclaimed, climbing from the buggy.

"Oh. It inside in de bedroom."

"Come now, Gideon." Professor Moeller said with a twinkle of the eye.

The gentleman rapped on the door with the head of his cane. As we waited for the door to open, the professor whistled a tune. I remember that I was a bit repulsed by the jovial nature of my companion. Even though he didn't know Mr. Janus, I thought a more somber attitude was in order. At the time I supposed that this was just another of my mentor's eccentricities.

Penny answered the door and let us in. Mrs. Janus was seated at the kitchen table drinking a cup of coffee. The widow was hardly the frantic mess Winston Jeffers had described (though of course he had gotten his information second-hand himself). Her eyes were glassy and her demeanor solemn but she was a long way from "frantic."

"Massa Gid'in. Hallo, sir. Come on in," Penny said quietly.

I paid my respects to Mrs. Janus, who politely nodded her reply. The professor introduced himself and asked the widow if he might take a seat. As they spoke, I pulled Penny aside.

"Penny, what happened?"

"Well, sir. We tinks de Massa go out fishin' dis mornin' an fall out de boat and drown."

"How is your mistress holding up?"

"She okay. She took a big dose of laudanum."

The Janus's certainly did not have a storybook marriage. However, I found it hard to believe that she did not mourn the

136

loss of her companion. I therefore convinced myself that the opium was the reason for her lethargy.

I was interrupted from my conversation with Penny as the professor beckoned me to follow him. We went into the bedroom, and there lying on the bed was the lifeless form of Henry Janus.

Professor Moeller closed the door behind us. We stood before the body in what I originally thought was silent reverence, until I glanced in the direction of my mentor. He was surveying the corpse intently.

"See here," he said in a hushed tone. "Look at this bruise on the temple."

There was indeed a large, severe bruise on the man's right temple. It looked as though the skull had been fractured.

The professor's next action took me completely by surprise. He leaned over the bed, folded both of his hands, and pushed down strenuously on the dead man's abdomen. He then put on his spectacles and leaning very close to Janus's face, examined his lips.

I stood dumbfounded at the professor's inexplicable action. Suddenly, he motioned me to follow him out of the room. We bid a hurried farewell to the poor widow and left the house. Once outside the professor related the content of his conversation with Mrs. Janus.

"Our good lady in there says that her husband often went fishing before she arose. It appears that he did so this morning, but drowned in the process. I told her who I was and asked if I might have a moment to examine the body, given that I was scientist of sorts. She had no objections."

"But what were you doing to him?" I blurted out impatiently.

"Ah," he chuckled. "Perhaps you will figure it out after you've read the Poe stories." He continued, "We need to speak with this 'Cy'. Mrs. Janus said that he is the one who discovered the body."

137

We walked over to the simple shack that was occupied by the father and son, and rapped on the door.

"Come on in!" was shouted from the interior. Inside both Gus and Cy were seated at a crude table, drinking a cup of cider. Both immediately stood respectfully as we entered. "Oh hallo, massas. What ken we do fo you?" the elder asked.

"Cy is it correct that you found your Master's body?" my teacher queried.

"Yas, sir."

"Well do come with us out to the pond. We would very much like to hear what happened."

The younger man led the way to the edge of the bridge. He explained that he found his master's body about six that morning, pinned against the lower dam.

"Where was the boat?" the professor asked.

"It was over yonder, in dem weeds," he said, indicating the eastern side of the lake. "See. It still dare." The boat was visible among the high grass on the opposite shore.

"Could your master swim?" the professor continued.

"Yas sir."

"Well how do you suppose he drowned then?"

"Me an my Pappy tinks dat he was standin' in de boat tryin' to make a tough cast, and dat he fall an bust his head on de boat. If he knocked out, it don't matter a lick how good he can swim!"

The professor smiled at this explanation. "Cy, I am aware of the fact that the body was found sucked against the lower dam, but was it floating, or several feet below the surface?

I was perplexed by this odd question, but the slave quickly replied.

"It was on de top of de water."

"Thank you Cy. That will be all," Professor Moeller said, dismissing the slave.

As the servant ambled back to his hut the professor turned to me.

138

"What do you think of Cy's analysis?"

"It seems plausible. Mr. Janus did have that ugly wound on his head."

The professor chuckled at my response. I was perplexed at this reaction. But he gave no indication as to his amusement. He merely nudged my arm with his cane and motioned for me to accompany him. "Let us take a stroll around this little pond and see if anything presents itself."

I did not understand what he could possibly mean as we began to circle the pool. We stopped at the dirt area nearest the house, and my teacher pointed to the ground.

"What do you see here, Gideon?" he asked.

I examined the ground where his cane was pointing. The area was where Janus kept his boat beached when he wasn't using it. The ground was muddy and obviously well traveled. A groove was apparent where the keel of the boat was pushed out into the water and footprints were embedded in the mud. I conveyed this general information to my tutor. He nodded and motioned us onward with a wave of his walking stick.

We continued our jaunt around the pond, stopping briefly at the lower dam where the body had been found. The flow of the water had instinctively brought the body to the southern extremity and the surge naturally pinned it against the orifice.

"Look there!" he said, pointing again with his cane. "What do you see?"

I made my observation from where we stood for fear of embroiling myself in the muck if I descended down to the water's edge. "More footprints," I replied.

"Gideon, you're grasp of the obvious is astounding," he said, a hint of disgust in his voice. "What *about* the footprints? Give me details," he urged, poking me with his cane.

"Well... These prints head down to the water and back again..."

"That's better," he replied in a more even tone. "What else?"

"Most pronounced are those leading to the water's edge. These..." I pointed to the marks heading away from the lake. "...are not as well defined, but still clear."

"Very good. Very good." He amused himself with another chuckle but without a word of explanation for me. "What about those?" he asked, pointing to another set of prints that I had not seen. These were on the opposite side of the dam.

"Hmm, well they are similar to the ones on this side in that they lead to the water's edge and back again. It appears that they are more distinct leading back up from the pond."

"I concur," he announced curtly and somewhat cryptically. "Come this way, my lad," he said before abruptly walking off.

I followed him along the shoreline until we reached the weeded area where the boat lay. Climbing through the high grass, we reached the craft. The professor examined it thoroughly but silently. I was inclined to ask exactly what he was looking for but his intent focus prevented me from doing so. Suddenly he stomped off, an aloof concentration upon his features. We continued around the remainder of the lake, the professor still in his silent, contemplative mood. My tutor did not find anything else worth noting, or at least nothing he felt like sharing.

Abruptly Professor Moeller stated that he did not think there was anything else to see and that he would be returning to Fincastle directly as he had some work to do on his botanical samples. I suppose that he detected the confused expression on my face. He laughed and patted me on the back. "Read the book, Gideon. Read the book. After you have done so, come into town on Thursday morning and we will discuss things further." The professor winked at me and was off.

I deposited the volume in my saddlebag and mounted Ajax. I had to wait to cross the narrow span that bridged the dene since

Mr. Jervis had arrived with his hearse. He nodded somberly as he passed me. His vehicle creaked by, a crude pine box in its bed.

I arrived back at The Copper Beeches to find that the news of Mr. Janus's demise had not yet reached the plantation. I found Uncle Robert in his library, intoxicated. I dreaded breaking the news to him while he was in such a state.

"Uncle Robert..." I said, after asking permission to sit.

"Yes. Gideon what is it." He poured himself another glass. By this time he had abandoned any inclination to hide his addition.

"Mr. Janus has drowned."

My Uncle looked down at the floor for a few moments, then looked at me and forced a smile. "That is sad. So many friends gone..." he trailed off and gazed out the window. I left him to his commiseration. He and Janus were more neighbors than friends, and although Janus's passing could not be considered a severe blow, it furthered the despondent sorrow that had grown to encompass him.

I rode out to the field to make sure all was in order. As usual, Bartholomew had things well in hand. I gave him the news about Janus, which was overheard by Ulysses and Cicero who were standing nearby. I caught a look of alarm on Ulysses' face. He was evidently concerned that this sad event might affect his ability to see his wife. Whenever a master dies the chief concern of his slaves is that the heir will sell them away from their family. I made a mental note to inquire of Mrs. Janus what her intensions were regarding Penny. I was about to leave when I noticed that Jeremy was limping.

"What happened to you?" I asked.

"Nothin' Massa. I fell down. Dat's all," replied the feisty slave.

"He says he fell in de barn," Bartholomew broke in. "But I tinks dat lazy polecat jus' tryin' to git out o' work again." He

141

raised his hand as if to strike, and Jeremy scurried back to work. "I tells you Massa. I wish you'd let me whip him. He a real scoundrel. I had to bust him upside de head jus' yesterday."

"No. No whipping..." I commanded, recalling the torture I witnessed at the Jeffers plantation. "...but feel free to punch his face if he gives you any trouble."

I completely trusted Bartholomew and knew that he would only strike if need be. Jeremy had always been the laziest of our people, and since Uncle Robert's decline he had gotten worse.

After dinner I began reading the selections from *Tales of the Grotesque and Arabesque*. I sat on the front porch in a rocker, good old Jack at my feet. I examined the stories the professor had enumerated. The first in the list was *The Gold Bug*. I opened to the appropriate page and began the tale.

The story revolved around a well educated and formerly wealthy man named William Legrand who had fallen on hard times and secluded himself on a barrier island off the coast of South Carolina. As the tale unfolds, Legrand is bitten by a gold-colored beetle and happens upon an encrypted message near the remains of an ancient boat.

As I read, I found myself mesmerized by the suspenseful nature of the story as the protagonist intricately weaves together a number of nebulous clues. Ultimately Legrand's ability to decipher the puzzle leads him to a treasure trove of gold and jewels.

The sun had nearly set by the time that I had finished the story. I was squinting laboriously in the dim light, but had become so entranced by the tale that I did not want to interrupt my reading, even long enough to move inside. I had never read such a story. Two elements in particular had drawn me in: the mystery and its solution. The mystery of the gold bug kept me riveted, and the scientific method employed in breaking the code aroused my own analytical nature.

142

I patted Jack good night and went to the kitchen. I had Covey fix me a cup of coffee, as I could not wait to begin the next story. I took my mug and went toward the parlor, but stopped just outside the door. Many a night this room had been the scene of reading and discussion sessions between mother, my uncle and me. As I peered in, I could see Uncle Robert seated before a dim fire, tankard in hand. I decided to retire to my room instead. Once upstairs I seated myself in a chair by the window. I lit the lamp on the table beside me, and secured the glass shade over the flame to protect it from the warm breeze that was billowing the curtains. I opened to *The Murders in the Rue Morgue*.

This story was no less mesmerizing than the last. It shared some of the characteristics of *The Gold Bug* as it relied on the protagonist's analytical intellect to solve the mystery. Again an unnamed narrator tells the tale. He begins by describing the powers of analysis and uses the game of whist as an example. He concludes that a good analyst will win the game by knowing whether his opponents have a good set of cards or not. He can ascertain this knowledge by carefully observing their every move. The narrator adds that an analyst is always ingenious, but an ingenious person (like the chess player) is not always a good analyst.

The aforementioned thought intrigued me greatly. I had often been called "a genius" (though I humbly admit this might be a great exaggeration), but as the narrator explained, that did not necessarily make me a good "analyst." Perhaps this was the lesson the professor had intended I learn? The narrator informs that he will use a real-life example to illustrate the powers of analysis. He goes on to tell of an event that occurred in Paris.

There had been a very violent and grotesque double murder in the "Rue Morgue," or "Rue Street" as we would say in English, which had stymied the local officials. Try as they might, they could not figure how, why, or by whom the gristly crime and been committed. Although several neighbors had heard a disturbance, no one had witnessed anything out of the ordinary.

The narrator is the companion of an eccentric fellow called C. August, Dupin. Dupin possesses exceptional skill in analytical perception and in addition is described as having and extraordinary imagination. In utilizing these gifts the protagonist solves the mysterious murders and clears an acquaintance who had been falsely accused.

It was after midnight by the time I finished the story. I had read it straight through, just as I had *The Gold Bug*. Just as with the previous selection, I was entranced by both the mystery and Dupin's means of solving it. I shut the book and extinguished the lamp; yet I could not sleep. I wondered what the professor's motive had been in directing me toward Poe's work. Was he insinuating that there was something sinister in the death of Mr. Janus? I replayed every moment spent at Deep Dene that day, but try as I might, I could not uncover anything of any significance. Perhaps I was still too adept at chess, and not yet proficient enough at whisk. I hoped that I would get more clues when I read the final two stories.

CHAPTER 9

After breakfast I made the ritual ride out to the fields to "supervise" the slaves' activity. Of course Bartholomew had things in order, so I spurred Ajax off a few hundred yards and dismounted by a large sycamore. I unsaddled my trusty horse and allowed him to graze nearby as I reclined under the tree. I was impatient to continue my reading, and opened the volume to *The Purloined Letter*.

This story again featured the eccentric "analyst" C. Auguste Dupin as he is afforded another opportunity to upstage the Parisian Prefect of Police. The tale is told by the same narrator from the previous story. He relates that the prefect paid them a visit to seek advice regarding a case. Dupin tells the policeman that perhaps his error is that he has overlooked the obvious facts. This simplistic comment causes the prefect to burst into laughter before sharing the particulars with his host.

The case involved the theft of a letter from a wealthy woman and the subsequent blackmailing of the woman over the missive. In desperation the woman had enlisted the police, hoping to recover the damaging correspondence, but the prefect's efforts had come up short. He had a prime suspect, a Minister D--- , and had even gone as far as searching "D's" apartment; but to no avail. As with the case of in the Rue Morgue, Dupin triumphs in locating and retrieving the letter by employing logic, insight, and imagination.

I took note of two distinct points from *The Purloined Letter*. The first was an echo of one presented in *The Murders in the Rue Morgue*— when confronting an adversary, put yourself in your opponent's place. In the first story this was illustrated through the game of whist. This tale provided a more concrete illustration of this concept. The second point is the precept of not overlooking the obvious or as the more common saying goes: "to fail to see the forest for the trees."

I took a moment and stared past Ajax, off into the fields. I tried to connect these ideas with the death of my neighbor and my peculiar reading assignment. By now I definitely had the feeling that the professor was sending me a message, but I still could not bring it into focus. Finally I concluded that it would be a waste of time to ponder any further until I had read the final story.

The Mystery of Marie Roget is subtitled as *A Sequel to The Murders in the Rue Morgue*. Apparently I had read the stories out of order when I decided to tackle *The Purloined Letter* before this tale. Since this was termed a sequel, it obviously again featured the esteemed analyst C. Auguste Dupin. The now familiar narrator begins by explaining that after Dupin's success in solving the mystery at the Rue Morgue the Parisian police often implored his friend to help with difficult cases. One such circumstance surrounded the murder of young girl by the name of Marie Roget.

This selection was much less interesting than the preceding three. It was actually quite mundane and progressed very slowly. Any reader undertaking this story in hopes of entertainment might be disappointed; however the details surrounding the corpse immediately arrested my attention. You see, the body had been recovered from the Seine River.

My interest increased as I reached the point in the story where Dupin reviews the police report describing the particulars of the cadaver. The hair on the back of my neck stiffened as I read the description of the corpse: ...*the face was suffused with dark blood, some of which issued from the mouth. No foam was seen, as in the case of the merely drowned...* "No foam?" I gasped as a thought dawned on me. "Could this explain the

146

professor's minute examination of Janus's mouth?" I pondered, awestruck.

I excitedly continued reading, and quickly came upon another clue applicable to my neighbor's fate: *All experience has shown that drowned bodies, or bodies thrown into the water immediately after death by violence, require from six to ten days for sufficient decomposition to take place to bring them to the top of the water.*

The next several pages were filled with Dupin's intricate dissection of the varied newspaper accounts regarding the girl's demise. Using logic, he systematically dispels most of the papers' hypotheses. My eyes locked onto a particular one of these where Dupin scrutinizes the physics of when a body will and will not float. It is explained that if a corpse were thrown into a body of water *after* death had occurred it would not sink at all. I thought aloud, "Was this yet another clue?"

As I came to the end of the story, I marveled ad the deductive reasoning Dupin employed to solve the girl's murder. And I believed that I had obtained several more pieces of the puzzle concerning what had actually occurred at Deep Dene. Unfortunately, I still did not know how they fit together. I had to see the professor. I needed to dislodge him from his coy demeanor and get him to make his views plain. But how would I do this? I was still hampered by the respect he commanded, and I was in no position to make demands from my tutor. Also, if he was being purposely surreptitious, I was sure there was a reason and hence he may be adverse to a clear discussion of the topic. The next day was Thursday, so I would have my opportunity at our scheduled meeting.

That night I lay in bed mulling over the Poe stories and trying to relate them to the fate of poor Mr. Janus. Outside, the crickets chirped and the locust buzzed in the trees. The symphony of insects had nearly lulled me to sleep when I burst back to consciousness with a start. A terrible thought entered my mind just as I was crossing the threshold of slumber. Why had the professor suspected foul play *before* we had even arrived at Deep Dene? Winston's account had hardly been suspicious; he merely stated that Mr. Janus had drowned. Yet, the professor was giddy with excitement to see the corpse. He gave me the book on the way *to* the Janus place. How could he have suspected anything sinister at that point? Could... could he have taken such a drastic step just to provide a mystery for use as a lesson? I struggled to shake the thought from my head. The old man had been kind, jovial, and endearing. How could I conjure up such thoughts? Added to this was the fact that I was getting too far ahead of myself. I had no evidence that anything bizarre had actually occurred at Deep Dene, and I had no idea why the professor had me read the Poe stories. Still... Dupin suggests that one must use the imagination...

The next morning Ajax carried me into Fincastle. Mrs. Evans showed me in and stated that the professor was not home at the moment but had left a message for me to wait, as he should be back shortly. I seated myself in his favorite chair and perused the volume I had brought back. I had not been waiting five minutes before the carriage drew up in front of the house.

"Hello, Gideon!" the old man boomed, as he burst into the room and deposited a small bundle of branches on the table. "I shall catalog these later," he announced to himself.

I stood respectfully when my tutor had entered, and endeavored to remove myself from his chair so that he could assume the seat himself but he arrested my progress.

"No, no. Sit. Sit," he commanded, as he pulled up a separate seat for himself.

We sat for a moment in an uncomfortable silence. Then I broke the deadlock by returning his text. "Oh. I almost forgot. Here is your book. Thank you."

"Did you read the selections?" he asked, with a flash of the emerald eyes.

"Yes."

"What do you think?" he asked, vaguely.

"Well," I replied a bit unsure of where he was headed, "they were quite good. I had never read any stories like them."

"I knew him you know."

"Who?" I asked confusedly.

"The author."

"Poe?"

"Yes. He attended the University of Virginia for a short time. I was just beginning my teaching there, and we spoke on a few occasions." The professor quickly turned from the author back to the literature. "Did you find anything relevant in the stories?"

"I am not sure..." I cautiously answered. "Do you think there is something suspicious about Mr. Janus's drowning?" I finally let the question loose.

"Oh he didn't drown," The professor calmly replied.

Ice shot up my spine. I stared back blankly, blinking my eyes in astonishment.

"How do suppose I came to that conclusion?" he asked, nudging my knee.

Against my will, my subconscious considered the fact that one who did the deed would know. I shook off the thought. "Well... I know that there was no foam about Mr. Janus's lips, and I read that foam would be present if he had drowned," I said, rather unsteadily.

"Yes. Yes. Good. But couldn't Cy or his wife have wiped his mouth? The absence of foam is a good starting point. What other indicators are there?" He leaned in toward me.

I reflected again. "Hmm. The body was found floating, and if Dupin is to be believed, a drowning victim would not float, at least not until decomposition began."

149

"Excellent!" my mentor replied, as he slapped my knee. However there is still yet another indicator. Do you recall what I did when we examined the body?"

I tried to call to mind the procedure he had followed. "I remember you examining his lips, the bruise on his forehead, -- and you put pressure on his abdomen?"

"Yes. I applied force to his midsection. When I did so, what came out of his mouth?"

"Why, nothing."

"Exactly!" he smiled broadly. "Had he drowned, his lungs would have filled with water. Pressing on the abdomen expels approximately a gallon of water from the lungs of a drowned man. Remember, after I did so, I carefully examined his lips. I did this to account for the possibility that in moving the body, Cy may have applied force to Mr. Janus's abdomen and expelled the water. However, had he done so, a small amount of water would have remained in the dead man's windpipe and settled back to the lungs. But-- no water was found whatsoever!"

"If he did not drown, what was the cause of death?"

"That is a good question. First let us examine what we know." He sat back in his chair. "Cy and Gus assumed that their master was fishing and that he slipped when making a cast, hit his head, tumbled overboard and drowned. This was a fair assumption for them to make, *or a clever story for them to concoct...*" he said, casting a sly look in my direction, "...but we have already determined that at least part of it is flawed, since Janus did not drown. What other possibilities are there?"

I thought for a moment. "I suppose that their scenario could still be true excepting the cause of death. Perhaps he was indeed trying to make a cast, slipped and banged his head, killing him before he fell into the water."

"Not a bad line of reasoning," he tapped his fingertips together. "However the wound on the temple provides a problem. First, if Janus had stumbled and struck his head on the

150

boat, he could not do so with any great amount of force. Yet when I examined the wound, it was quite obvious that the blow had been considerable. To inflict such a severe wound he would have had to fall from a height of twenty feet rather than merely stumble in the craft. Also, we both looked at the boat, and there was not a mark of blood on it."

"Perhaps his heart had attacked him and he was dead before he fell and hit his head!" I impetuously exclaimed.

"Gideon!" he laughed. "We just established that the blow was too brutal to have been caused by a tumble on the boat!"

I turned red, ashamed at my foolishness.

"There is also evidence that he was never in the boat at all."

My pulse quickened.

"Where was the body recovered?" he asked.

"From the lower dam."

"Where was the boat recovered?"

"From the weeds on the eastern shore."

"In *The Purloined Letter*, Dupin cautions that the analyst must often take a step away from the scene and view the larger picture so as not to lose himself in the details. If Janus fell from the boat, how is it that he and the boat did not end up in the same place?" he asked, nudging my leg.

I scratched my head. "I don't know," I replied, completely confused by this unexpected twist.

"Oh come now, Gideon! You are capable of better than that!" he chastised. "Think scientifically. How did the body end up at the dam?"

"The current brought it there."

"Wouldn't the boat end up there as well?" he asked.

"I would certainly think so."

"And yet it did not. Rather, it was embedded in the weeds on the eastern shore. There are two things that influence a boat's drift. The first you have already named-- the current. What is the second?"

151

"Wind!" the answer burst from my lips, as I recalled the violent windstorm early the morning Janus had been found.

"Precisely!" He punctuated his statement by pointing at me with his forefinger.

"So, the boat was pushed by the windstorm early that day..." I scratched my head. "But if the wind was strong enough to propel the boat, shouldn't it have also driven the body into the weeds as well?"

"Undoubtedly."

I was stumped again, but my tutor came to the rescue.

"Let us abandon the corpse of poor Mr. Janus for the moment and concentrate on the boat. You were apparently awake when the windstorm hit?"

"Oh yes."

"Me too," he chuckled. "I thought the roof was going to blow off! Do you recall the hour the wind began to blow?"

"Yes. It was about four a.m."

"Do you recall when it died down?" he followed up.

"Things quieted down about an hour later."

"You have just answered the question of when the boat was launched. It was set adrift no earlier than four and no later than five. We may not yet know when your neighbor entered the pond, but we certainly know when he did not. He must have entered the fishing hole either before or after the intense, but brief, windstorm."

I was disappointed that I had been unable to deduce the aforementioned facts for myself. I am sure that my facial expression betrayed my consternation.

"Gideon my boy, you are still looking at things through the eyes of the chess player!" he said, quietly laughing to himself.

"Perhaps you will do better with the next clue," he said, poking my knee. "Reiterate what you observed about the footprints."

I felt horrible at my lack of success thus far. I furrowed my brow. "Well, we found footprints in three different areas. The first were at the boat landing." I thought for a moment, but could not recall anything significant about these marks. "Next there were the two sets that went down to the water and back. I recollect that the first set was deeper when going toward the pond than in returning and that the second set was more depressed when headed *away* from the water."

"You were astute enough to observe these particulars? Excellent! Dupin would now suggest that you use your imagination to explain the cause." He flashed the green eyes in my direction.

I thought for a moment. I may have even closed my eyes, but I cannot recall exactly. "Weight! In the first instance the weight was greater when going down to the shoreline. In the second case the weight was greater upon the return. Something was carried to the water and deposited, and then retrieved!"

"Bravo, my lad! Bravo! Now take the supposition a step further. What was this mysterious item of considerable weight?"

"Mr. Janus," I concluded, in a near whisper.

"Now it is most likely that the second set belonged to Cy as he retrieved the body. You can ask him if that is where he ascended the bank when you go back to Deep Dene."

I was immersed in thought so it took a second for me to comprehend what the professor had just said. "Huh? Go back to Deep Dene?"

"Yes. Here," he said, handing me a pad and pencil from his desk. "Though your scrutiny of the footprints was sharp enough to reveal their depth, you missed another distinctive point. It has been warm and the sun will have baked them, so they will be even easier to examine. Sketch what you find on that paper and then come back tomorrow."

With that Professor Moeller abruptly replaced the chair upon which he had been sitting and went to the table and began

153

cataloging the samples he had brought in that morning. Confused, I rose to leave. I took a step toward my teacher and opened my mouth to ask a question, but was silenced as he waved me off without even looking up. "Off you go now. Tomorrow. We will talk again tomorrow." I ambled out the door in puzzlement.

I had wanted to query the professor about his premature suspicions about Mr. Janus's demise. Despite my best efforts, my apprehension about my teacher's possible role in the killing had only partially abated. Unfortunately, my eccentric mentor would have no further discussion on the subject. Therefore my misgivings would have to continue to simmer until our next meeting.

I decided that I should head to Deep Dene immediately. Although the sky was relatively clear, one never knows when it will rain, and I did not want to ruin my opportunity to re-inspect the footprints. As Ajax trotted out of Fincastle I mulled over the singular dialog the professor and I had just had. His approach was very much like that of Dupin in that the "solution" (if solution it was) was hatched miles from the actual scene of the misdeed. Like Poe's analyst he first obtained what facts were available then used his imagination to draw conclusions about his observations. Through our discussion he had led me to his own findings, and I must admit his ideas seemed sound. Yet, the case was incomplete. Dupin's investigations always led to a perpetrator. I would have to be sure to explore this point when I returned to see the professor tomorrow.

About halfway to the Janus place I turned off the road and directed Ajax through a thin strip of trees. Just on the other side of this grove was an apple orchard belonging to the O'Sullivans. I was famished and I was sure that the one Catholic family in the area would not begrudge a hungry Protestant silencing the rumbling in his stomach with a single apple.

154

By the time I reached Deep Dene I had devoured the fruit. It was not yet fully ripe, and thus a bit sour, but as the saying goes "beggars cannot be choosers." As I crossed the wooden bridge, I tossed the core into the pond. I kept my eye upon it as I approached the house. It made a slow but sure beeline for the lower dam.

As I dismounted, Gus emerged from behind the house and hitched my mount.

"Is Mrs. Janus at home?" I asked.

"Yas, but she asleep. Dat opium, you know. I hopes when she done de bottle dat she not git anoder one!" the concerned slave replied, furrowing his brow.

"Well I'm going to take a little walk around the pond. I'm sure she won't mind. Where is Cy?"

"He off pickin' berries."

"Please fetch him for me."

"Yas sir."

I expected the elder slave to be curious as to the nature of my unexpected arrival, but he betrayed no signs of any interest at all. As he went off to retrieve his son, I headed for the small clearing where the boat was beached.

The boat had been recovered from the weeds and again resided in its usual spot. This added newer, fresher, footprints to the mix. Unfortunately the newer prints, (presumably made by Gus or Cy when they recovered the boat) had obscured the ones that the professor and I had previously observed. Disheartened but not distressed, I continued my advance toward the other two sets.

The path I took first brought me to the "second set," (those thought to be from Cy when he retrieved Mr. Janus's body). I clamored down the bank, sketch-pad in hand, and minutely observed the marks. They were approximately ten inches in length, and plain in appearance. By plain I mean that the shoe did not possess a heel, and both the left and the right foot left the

155

same impression. This fact added evidence that suggested that these were indeed Cy's footmarks. Slave's shoes are not custom-made by a cobbler. Rather they are bought in bulk from northern factories and are interchangeable on either foot. It took but a minute to sketch the markings since as I indicated, they were so plain.

Next I crossed the lower dam and headed toward the first set of prints. According to the professor's logic, these were made by whoever tossed the corpse into the pond. Now that I was focused on detail, I made clearer observations than on my first trip. This time I noticed that the marks that led down to the water were different from those that headed away. The prints that marked the path toward the pond were small and "U" shaped. The ones returning were also small but triangular. However, this puzzled me for only a moment. I set aside my observation lens and switched to that of imagination. I closed my eyes and tried to picture the mysterious individual as he dumped the body and then made his retreat. I quickly perceived the reason for the difference. At this spot, the bank was quite steep. The "U" shaped prints were the result of the owner applying pressure to his heels to prevent a rapid descent that would throw him headlong into the pond. The triangular prints were caused by the opposite effect; the perpetrator had stridden on his toes in order to ascend the steep incline.

The fact that the culprit had left marks from only his heels and toes prevented me from being able to either confirm or deny whether slave shoes had made them. This determination had easily been rendered on the first set of prints, but here, the absence of any instep markings foiled a similar identification as I could not discern if both shoes were interchangeable. This same fact also thwarted any attempt at determining the size of the shoe since only half of the print was visible at any given time. However, there was yet another distinction to be observed. In closely examining the marks I noticed the right heel had a

156

horizontal line running across it. The line was about a quarter of an inch in width and spanned the entire width of the heel area. I postulated that the shoe in question had a crack or cut in that portion of the sole.

I was just finishing sketching the prints when Cy came jogging up. I questioned as to where he had retrieved the body, and he confirmed the scenario already outlined by the professor. I next asked him about the markings now in front of us. The bewildered expression on his face led me to conclude that he was being truthful when he stated that he had never seen them and did not know their origin.

Cy walked with me as I returned to reclaim my mount. Gus also ambled up as I prepared to leave. I posed a question that I had conjured on the walk back around the pond. "Where does your master keep his fishing tackle?"

Gus, always the more talkative of the two, replied, "Over in yonder shed." He pointed to a small building attached to the side of the barn.

"Show me," I commanded.

The two slaves led me to the shed and indicated a rack that held several fishing poles. "Are any missing?" I asked.

"No sir, dey all dare."

My face lit up. I had added evidence to our collection by proving that Janus had not 'gone fishing.' If he had, a pole would have been missing! Unfortunately my elation was short lived.

"You see dat one." Cy said pointing to the one on the bottom. "Dat's de one I pull out o' de boat when I found it in de weeds."

"Oh," I replied, somewhat dejected. I returned to Ajax, followed by the two servants. I was about to climb into the saddle when a thought crossed my mind. Turning to the pair I asked, "May I see the soles of your shoes?" I said this in a tone that resembled an order more than a request (such was the habit of dealing with slaves).

Gus laughed. "You sure is an odd one, Massa!" He complied, turning around and lifting first his left, then his right foot. The tell-tale mark was not present. Cy was more wary; one might even say "suspicious," but he too performed the routine, and he too was exonerated.

As I rode off, I overheard the father and son discussing my strange request. "Dey say he de smartest boy in de county, but I doesn't know if maybe he ain't as smart as he is touched," Gus joked to his boy. This comment did not draw my attention as much as the fact that the son did not return the laughter. I deduced that he either knew that there was a method to my madness or perhaps my actions had caused him some worry.

In concluding my expedition I was only a bit wiser than when I had begun. If the professor was correct, the set of prints on the near side of the dam belonged to the person who had deposited the body. Due to the mark on the heel I now had a link to that person. However, who could it be?

More questions quickly followed. Did the person who disposed of the body kill Mr. Janus? We had established that Janus had not drowned and that the aforementioned person had placed him in the pond. It is almost certain that the injury to his head had been the cause of death, but was that injury the result of assault or accident? If murder had occurred, was the owner of the mysterious footprints the assassin?

These questions plagued me the rest of the day and throughout the night. My hope was that when I went to see the professor in the morning he could shed some more light upon the mystery.

CHAPTER 10

I returned to Mrs. Evans' boarding house the next morning. As I entered the parlor I instinctively looked to the professor's favorite chair, but it was empty. The old man was across the room, hard at work on his botanical classifications. I remember that I found it considerably odd that the professor could shift gears so easily. One moment he was entirely embroiled in the mystery of Mr. Janus's death and the next he had put it completely out of his mind and turned his attention to his hunt for the delicious blackberries.

"Hello there, Gideon. I see that you have your sketch pad. Good." He hastily concluded the entry he was making in his journal, crossed the room and plopped into his favorite chair. As I pulled up a seat he took the drawings from my hand.

"Hmm. Yes. Yes. This is the exact recollection I have in my mind's eye," he said, examining the sketches through his spectacles. "Yesterday you deduced that these prints," he said, as he held up one of the drawings, "had been made by someone carrying a heavy object *from* the water. Did you confirm that they belonged to Cy?" he asked.

"Yes. He admitted that they were his, and as you can see by the drawing, they are clearly slave's shoes." I said, pointing out the aforementioned indicators.

"Excellent work!" he praised.

"Also I examined his shoes and they correspond to the size of those prints."

"Very thorough, my boy. Poe would be proud!" he nudged my knee. "Now let us move on to this other set. They of course present more mystery." He shuffled the papers to bring another sketch to the forefront. "We have already concluded that these

159

marks were left by whoever dumped your poor neighbor in the pond. What did you discover on your more recent examination?"

First, I retraced my conclusions regarding the strange "U" and triangular prints.

"Well done," he beamed.

I was beginning to recover from the feelings of inadequacy I harbored from our last interview. With my confidence climbing I pointed to the odd slash across the right heel. Next I proudly related how I had examined the shoes of both Gus and Cy.

The "slash" had undoubtedly caught the professor's eye on the first trip to Deep Dene, and he was pleased though not surprised, that I found this rather obvious mark. However he was impressed that I demonstrated both the insight and temerity to command the slaves to show me their footwear.

Next I sheepishly related my failure with the fishing pole, but the professor was not critical. He chuckled and reminded me that nothing could ever be proven without first experimenting with various postulates. He bolstered my confidence by stating that my idea was an excellent one. Had the pole been present in the shed, but not replaced, it would have added further credence to the conclusion that Janus had not been fishing. But the presence of the rod in the boat does not itself guarantee that its owner had been using it that morning. He added a word of caution. "Where you went wrong my boy, was allowing your emotions to interfere with your conclusions. As I said, your *inquiry* was well founded, therefore whatever the result, you should not have been dejected."

I had been very anxious to meet with the professor in hopes that he would reveal the identity of the mysterious figure who deposited Mr. Janus in the pond, if his own perceptions reached that far. So, as subtly as I was able, I tried to direct the conversation in that direction.

160

"Professor... do you have any idea who these prints belong to?" I asked, holding up the sketch of the unidentified marks.

My tutor laughed aloud, but did not answer. He looked out the window for a long moment and then he changed the course of the discussion.

"Let us review what we know. Janus did not drown. He died from a severe blow to the head. Despite the presence of the rod in the boat, he had not been fishing-- In fact he had not been in the boat at all. The boat had been launched between four and five in the morning, and Janus had been deposited in the pond either before four or after five. Cy recovered the body and neither he nor his father were the person who had deposited it in the water. Does that sound right so far?" he smiled, flashing his green eyes in my direction.

"Yes," I replied, going over the details in my head.

"Although we are sure that Mr. Janus was purposely placed into the pond, we do not know if his death was intentional or not. Here we must make a rather large supposition. What do you think; was he murdered or merely the victim of an accident?"

I thought for a moment. I definitely had my own opinion on the subject, but I did not want to make a wrong move and disappoint my mentor. Finally I decided that I had to answer since I'd already kept him waiting a half a minute. "I believe that he was murdered." I replied with a confident voice but an admittedly uneasy heart.

"I agree," the professor returned with a gleam in his eye. "Why do you feel as you do?"

I had no time to formulate an articulate answer, so I plodded ahead with what I had already surmised. "Well, it seems unlikely that anyone would take such pains to try to cover up an accident. Also, I have turned over in my mind many scenarios whereby Mr. Janus could have obtained the fatal blow to his head at such an odd hour of the morning. I am always led to a circumstance of violence."

161

"I am glad to hear that you have begun tapping into your imagination! Perhaps you will become a formidable whisk player yet. I concur with your deduction that it would be very unlikely that your neighbor met with such a violent accident, and even stronger evidence is present in the surreptitious events that put Janus at the dam. The two together definitely suggest murder and an attempt at concealing that deed."

I was relieved that the professor agreed not only with my conclusion, but also with the means by which I reached it.

"Now we must turn to the question of whether the person who killed Mr. Janus was the same individual who deposited him in the water. What are your feelings upon this point?" he asked, with a nudge of my knee.

From the time that I came to the conclusion that Janus had been murdered, I had assumed that the killer had dumped the body. Suddenly the professor presented another possibility. I thought for a few moments before answering.

"I am of the opinion that the murderer is also the one who undertook the act of concealing the crime. Janus was killed sometime during that early morning, and we only identified one set of footprints where the body had been cast off. If another person, or more than one person, had committed the crime I think there would have been two sets of prints. It would be much easier for two people to carry a body than just one. Also, it has been my experience that the greater the number to keep a secret, the less likely it will be kept." I thought for a moment before continuing. "I suppose that there may have been a conspiracy but it doesn't seem likely." I looked up at my tutor. "Professor... do you think that we should make our suspicions known?"

"To whom? You and I appear to be the only vestige of intelligence in the area!" he laughed. "No, no. You must continue with your investigation. If upon reaching a solution you deem it necessary to contact the constable or justice of the peace or whatever passes for the law out here, then at that point you should consider it."

Suddenly it was *my* investigation? I thought it odd and intimidating that the professor had unexpectedly bestowed such responsibility on me. However I did not dwell on this point. A solution did not appear imminent and if and when it did, I was confident that my mentor would not abandon me. The professor was right, though. Before his arrival I was considered the oddball due to my intellect, and his eccentricities made my own pale in comparison. It would not be wise to air our ideas at present.

"We have now concluded that the owner of that flawed right shoe is the murderer. Given our progression of logic and the infusion of supposition, it is a logical assumption to make. Now if you recall, in *The Mystery of Marie Roget*, Dupin instructed that the police should concentrate on finding the rudderless boat, which would in turn lead them to the culprit. We could say the same of the flawed shoe. Find the shoe, and you find the murderer. However, it would be impossible to search the soles of every shoe in the county without having yourself committed to an asylum. Therefore, you must narrow your search. I suspect that your next step should be to survey the townsfolk and try to determine if your neighbor had any enemies. If one or more possibilities present itself, the shoe may supply the corroborative evidence."

Thus my instructor had given me my new assignment, and having done so, he shooed me out the door performing one of his characteristic shifts back to a botanical researcher.

"Professor..." I tried again to broach the subject of his premature suspicion of murder. He again ignored me, waving me away with his hand. However, this time I asserted myself. "Professor!" I commanded his attention. However, the old man was not startled by my exclamation. Rather he smiled and directed his green eyes directly upon me.

163

"Yes?" he smirked.

"I'm sorry…" I sheepishly addressed him. "But I have been troubled by something. How… or rather why, did you suspect foul play?" My eyes implored the Professor not only for *an* answer, but one that would exonerate him.

My mentor laughed, removing his spectacles. "I'm the one who should be sorry my boy. What must you have thought?" He laughed again, slapping his knee. "One day at Drower's I ran into your Mr. Janus and we began to speak of fishing. Well, actually he was discussing fishing while I was interested in the species of the fish. Our discussion turned into a disagreement over which freshwater fish was the most agile. Your neighbor asserted that the long slender body of the pickerel made it the most nimble where I contended that salmon's ability to swim upstream demonstrated that it was clearly the most sprightly. Your Mr. Janus considered himself quite an expert on fish…" he trailed off in a chuckle. "He became a bit irritated and stated that *he* could out swim a 'damned salmon!'"

The aforementioned encounter obviously amused the professor. He continued, "So you see I knew that Janus could swim. Indeed he fancied himself quite a good swimmer by his boast!" he laughed again. "Thus I found drowning an unlikely cause of death. At that time I did not know that anything sinister had transpired but I was in a suspicious mood given my reading material (the Poe book) and I was excited to at least investigate. Just as I could have been wrong about your horse's name, I could have been wrong here as well. But I wasn't…" he waved a finger contemptuously in my direction while winking his left eye.

"Alright! Off you go now. I must get back to my botany. Go and see if you can find any Janus haters!" He laughed again, shaking his head as he went back to work.

The explanation, and my teacher's casual demeanor in expressing it, assured me that he had played no part in the murder. However, he had quarreled with Mr. Janus not long before his death. Could he still be linked in some way to his demise? As I stepped onto the porch a sudden thought exploded in my mind.

I turned to the professor's slave, who sat gently rocking in a chair, eyes closed, with his right ankle perched upon his left knee. Could Darius have killed Janus to avenge the dispute with his master? Slowly, and as silently as possible, I crept down the steps and around to the side of the porch. I peeked between the balusters to examine the exposed sole of his right shoe. Relief and frustration played an emotional tug of war as it became obvious that the professor's man was not the owner of the scarred shoe.

I sagged onto a nearby tree stump. How was I to ascertain if any others had a dispute with the dead man without arousing suspicion? In my mind I rolled over the motives for murder. I had read a plethora of classical literature where murders had been central to the theme. Revenge, love, money, passion were all common sources for the rage needed to kill. As I looked up, I saw Mr. Drower's store down the street. Money. Perhaps it was money. I walked over to the store and mounted the steps.

Once inside I asked Mr. Drower if I could examine our account in his book. The German was his usual irritable self, but I sensed a sliver of sympathy. I deduced that he was of the opinion that I was checking up on my uncle, since by this time Uncle Robert's addiction was well known. He handed over the ledger and then went back to stocking a shelf behind the counter. Slyly I turned the page to expose Mr. Janus's account. He was of course much poorer than we were, but his expenditures were also more modest. It appeared that Janus had not accrued any great debt at Drower's and that he had been living within his means. I thanked the cantankerous shopkeeper and left the store.

I could not think of any other way to pursue my latest assignment without exciting mistrust. I was about to climb aboard Ajax when Mrs. Evans beckoned me to the kitchen for a candied apple. Suddenly I had an idea. No one was more versed in the business of others than Mrs. Evans. I thanked her for the treat and deviously turned her attention to Mr. Janus.

"Ma'am, do you know when Mr. Janus' funeral will be held?" I of course was already aware of the fact that it was to be the following day, but I thought it an innocent way of engaging her in conversation.

"Yes, its tomorrow," she stated, in her matter-of-fact countenance.

"I suppose it will be a well attended event," I said, trying to lead the old woman on.

"Them Janus's kinda kept to themselves. But they were well-liked so I suppose he will fill a church as well as another."

That was all I needed. Had there been a bit of scandal known in town the old hen would have been privy to it and her nature would have forbid her from keeping it quiet.

I rode from town eating my treat, and wondering how to proceed. The next day I would attend the service for Mr. Janus, and while in town I would pay a visit to the professor for a bit of guidance.

The following morning we attended the funeral of Henry Janus. Our entire family was present, and Covey had come as well to supervise my cousins. Much to my relief, Uncle Robert was unusually lucid. I found it surprising that he was sober. Not only was this a rare event these days, but an event as melancholy as this undoubtedly increased his sorrow and thus his penchant for drink. The service was early, which led me to believe that my uncle had not had sufficient time to become inebriated.

The funeral was tasteful and short. After the service concluded, my uncle busied himself conversing with several of our neighbors. This gave me the opportunity to run down the street and pay a visit to the professor. I was anxious to obtain some more direction, since I had hit a wall in my quest for suspects. Unfortunately, my teacher was not at home.

As I approached I saw my uncle talking with the widow Janus. By the time I reached them, she had gone off to bury her husband in the church cemetery. We climbed aboard the coach and I cracked the reigns, spurring the team homeward.

"Gideon," Uncle Robert said, "When we get back I want you to ride out to the fields and talk to Bartholomew. Tell him that after they have concluded for the day, he is to have Jeremy pack all of his possessions. He is to take him to Deep Dene. Jeremy is now the property of Mrs. Janus."

The news struck me like a thunderbolt. "You sold Jeremy to Mrs. Janus?" I asked in shock.

"Not exactly. With Henry dead Mrs. Janus will need another set of male hands at Deep Dene. Unfortunately she is not financially able to purchase another slave. So I suggested a trade: Jeremy for Penelope."

My jaw dropped and then my heart warmed. The aforementioned transaction demonstrated a resurgence of my uncle's best qualities. He had found a way to help out a neighbor in need, and in a way that simultaneously benefited The Copper Beeches. Though a healthy male like Jeremy was worth more than Penny, Ulysses would be reunited with his wife at long last, and, now any children they produced would be ours rather than the property of Mrs. Janus. Also we got rid of Jeremy. Though he was an able bodied young man, he was lazy and I'm sure Bartholomew was tired of prodding him to work.

My uncle continued his instructions, "Be sure to let Bartholomew know that he has my permission to smack Jeremy around if he whines about this new arrangement. Conditions at Deep Dene are not nearly as pleasant as those at The Copper Beeches, so he may put up a fuss. Of course at the Janus place he will no longer be under Bartholomew's control and to Jeremy this may provide enough incentive to prevent him from complaining." My uncle furthered by stating that Bartholomew was to bring Penelope back with him on his return from the Janus farm.

I was beaming with excitement at our acquisition of Penny. I had quickly realized my folly when I had suggested to Ulysses that we might one day be able to bring his wife to The Copper Beeches. Now, quite unexpectedly, that flippant remark had come to fruition. In truth, I never understood why the Janus's kept Penny in the first place. Their crude cabin hardly required the attention of a domestic slave. In fact, petite little Penny was made to work in the fields alongside Cy and Gus. Another male slave would have been of much more use.

After we arrived home, I took the coach to the barn and stowed the horses in the stable. I then saddled and mounted my own horse and rode out to find our people. I trotted past the grove of maples and pines, through the village, and off toward the far field where I knew our slaves to be working.

I called Bartholomew away from his teams and gave him my uncle's instructions. A wide smile spread across the usually stoic slave driver's face, though he gave no other signs of elation. He merely answered with a "Yas sir!" I handed Bartholomew the pass my uncle had prepared and reminded him not to break the news to Jeremy until we had gotten a full day's work out of him.

I was about to ride off, but I could not resist informing Ulysses. I rode a good distance away from the slaves and then called him over. The industrious fellow reacted as most slaves did to such a summons--with suspicion. More often than not, an individual conference with a master forebodes either punishment or bad news. Ulysses warily approached, and appeared even more concerned when I got down off of my horse to talk to him. I cleverly maneuvered Ajax between our position the rest of the slaves in order to block our conversation from their view.

"Ulysses, I have called you over here to tell you something..." I said, in the most commanding voice I could muster. "...I have some news for you."

"Yas sir," he replied; his hat in hands and eyes cast downward in a penitent manner as he nervously pawed at the ground with his foot.

"You cannot speak of what I am about to tell you. Do you understand?" I continued.

"Yas sir," he submissively replied again.

"I don't want Jeremy to know this quite yet but you will no longer be sharing a cabin with him. We are moving someone else in with you."

"Okay, sir." I detected a hint of relief in this response.

"It is a female," I coyly continued, reminiscent of the old Uncle Robert.

This brought a shudder of fear upon the poor slave. Masters often tried to "breed" their slaves to force the production of more slaves for the plantation. "But sir... I's already married. I can't..." he trailed off and tears welled up in his eyes.

"Well then I guess I'll have to find another place for her, but I would have thought that you would have approved of us bringing Penny here to live at The Copper Beeches," I said quickly, as I thought it unfair to torture the poor soul further.

It took a moment for it to register, but as soon as it did, the tears that had formed from distress now flowed freely from joy. "Is it true, Massa?" he asked in disbelief.

"Yes." I smiled back.

He shook my hand vigorously and thanked me profusely. "Now listen. I can only go through with it if you keep quiet all day. We have traded Jeremy for her and I don't want him to suspect anything until Bartholomew informs him. Do you understand?"

"Yas Massa! I won't say a word!"

"Good. Contain yourself and you and your wife will be together by nightfall."

As I rode off toward the house I felt a degree of contentment that was far greater than any sentiment I had ever experienced. I had a warm feeling in my heart when I thought of being able to reunite two people who were obviously deeply in love. Ulysses' return to Botetourt County was itself astounding, but it was truly miraculous that they now would be able to live as a proper man and wife.

That evening I became embroiled in a duty I had unfortunately neglected as of late-- tutoring my cousins. I tried to make up for lost time and spent several hours poring over their lessons with them. I had intended on being on hand for Penny's arrival, but I lost all track of time and before I knew it, the hour of her appearance had passed. When I remembered, I thought about walking out to the village to welcome the new girl as well as wish the couple best tidings, but on reflection I thought it more respectful to allow the reunited their privacy in their first evening of their new life together.

After breakfast the next morning I jogged out to the village as our people were prepared to leave for the fields. I first stopped at Bartholomew's cabin and inquired how everything went in the slave exchange. He informed me that Jeremy first reacted with distain, hemming and hawing. However he quickly became resigned to his fate when Bartholomew told him that he could suggest that we send him to Chiltern Grange instead. This bluff had the desired effect as Jeremy had absolutely no desire to be owned by the draconian Winston Jeffers.

I was too late to stop in on Ulysses and Penny at their cabin, but I caught a glimpse of the pair as they ambled along in the procession toward the fields. The couple walked hand-in-hand, in apparent bliss despite the backbreaking labor that awaited them until sunset.

I was anxious to get into Fincastle and talk with the professor, but there were some matters that first needed attention. I spent the entire afternoon delving through the ledgers in my uncle's study. By now I had completely inherited the task of keeping the plantation's books. Unfortunately Uncle Robert had made quite a mess of several pages and I laboriously tried to decode his drunken entries and make sense of our assets.

We had just finished dinner when Zeke appeared at the back door. Apparently a mule had broken its leg and needed to be shot. Uncle Robert staggered into his study and unlocked the cabinet where he kept the guns. He took out a pistol and examined the chambers to make sure that it was loaded. He took a couple of steps before I stepped in his way.

"Uncle Robert...why don't you let me handle this?" I asked, considerably worried at the prospect of my intoxicated uncle handling a firearm.

A wry smile crossed his face as he handed me the revolver. "Yes. I'm sure that would be a better idea," he quietly said, as he patted me on the shoulder.

I asked Zeke where the injured animal lay and told him to saddle up Ajax. I drank down my glass of cider and quickly swallowed my last bit of dinner before heading out to the stable. I deposited the gun in the saddlebag and rode off in search of the wounded mule.

I found the unfortunate beast right where Zeke had directed. The mule had been pulling a plow when it stepped in a hole and stumbled, breaking its left rear leg nearly in two. It was a heart-wrenching sight. The poor animal was obviously in pain, yet kept following its natural instinct to stand. Unfortunately its afflicted leg could not support its weight and it kept falling back into the dust, the lower portion of the leg flailing about like a stick on a string.

The slaves had all retreated to a safe distance, but I needed their help. I did not want to take the shot from a distance and

171

increase the ill-fated mule's suffering by missing its head. It was thrashing about to such a great degree that I thought it unlikely that I could hit its skull, and I certainly did not want to shoot the poor beast in the body. Therefore I instructed several of the male slaves to jump on her the next time she fell. It took some harsh words to get the slaves to comply, as they were not anxious to receive a kick from the floundering beast. After several aborted attempts they were able to pounce on the animal. I strode up to it and looked into its wild eyes. I pulled the trigger and put the mule out of its misery.

Bartholomew instructed Zeke to bring up the wagon. I gave my assent in allowing the carcass to be brought to the village after the day's work was done so that they could butcher the meat and salvage the hide. However I also cautioned that before breakfast the next day they were to deposit the remains in the bone yard at the southeastern corner of the property.

I replaced the pistol in the saddlebag and remounted Ajax. I was about to return to the house when I stopped to watch the men load the heavy and awkward cargo into the bed of the wagon. It was such a difficult job that even Bartholomew was forced to join in. The slaves had to lower themselves to their knees to get their hands under the remains, and it was at this juncture that I caught sight of something that made my heart sink into my stomach. A heel with a slash across it. It was as plain as day. One of our own people had killed Mr. Janus! I was stricken with panic. I did not know how to proceed. I simply had to discuss this revelation with the professor. I bid a hasty farewell to Bartholomew and took off toward town. Dupin had explained that the solution was often hidden in plain sight. Just as the purloined letter had been right under the prefect's nose, the killer had been living on my own plantation.

By the time I arrived in Fincastle, poor Ajax was completely exhausted. I vaulted out of the saddle and leaped up Mrs.

172

Evans's steps two at a time. Without any feign of composure I banged on the front door.

"What in tarnation?!" the old lady exclaimed as she opened the door.

Forgetting my manners I rudely brushed past her, explaining as I entered. "I'm sorry ma'am is the professor in? I really need to see him." I was already halfway into the parlor by the time I finished this statement. Without even bothering to knock, I entered the room but found it vacant. "Will the professor be back shortly? Do you mind if I wait for him?" My questions followed directly on top of each other, hardly giving the landlady a chance to answer as she puffed after me.

"Now hold on there, Gideon!" she commanded, catching up.

My face went flush with embarrassment as I realized my inappropriate behavior.

"You may *not* wait for the professor," came the terse reply "because he has gone back east."

"Gone?" I nearly stammered incredulously. "When will he return?" I anxiously inquired.

"I don't think he *is* coming back," the landlady snapped.

"Not coming back?" I softly repeated in disbelief.

The old woman obviously felt a pang of sympathy for me as her tone softened considerably. "Yes." she said in more subtle tone, "He has gone. However, he left a letter for you. It is on the desk," she said, pointing into the parlor.

My shock was such that I sleep walked into the room in a daze. I picked up the envelope and sunk into the old man's favorite chair. I turned it over several times in my hands. My mood had changed from one of nervous excitement to extreme melancholy. I had come to feel a real affection for the man behind the bright green eyes. After my mother passed, I had been utterly dejected. Yet I was rescued out of this gloom when the old man came into my life. He had taken me under his wing and provided me with the academic companionship that I had

173

lost with my mother's death. He had become more than a companion though; he had challenged my intellect and fostered my growth both intellectually and morally. I had only known Professor Moeller a short time, but at that moment I felt as much despair as I have ever experienced.

I tore open the envelope and removed the folded piece of paper. It read:

My Dear Boy,

I apologize for my hasty departure. An express rider arrived with a message from the telegraph office in Roanoke. One of my colleagues from the university is heading a five-man panel due to attend a symposium at the Universiteit Leiden in The Netherlands and one of the members of the panel suddenly fell ill. He offered me the opportunity to replace the stricken professor and attend the conference in his stead. Unfortunately, I must leave immediately in order to make it to Norfolk in time to catch the ship. I will try to write you from the continent.

Remember my dear boy: Being intelligent is only half the battle. What will you do with your abilities? What impact will you make?

Sincerely,

Prof. William H. Moeller.

And so my education with Professor Moeller came to an abrupt end. I put the letter into my pocket and trudged out the door. The sun was setting as I mounted Ajax and set off for home. "How could he abandon me?" I angrily pondered. "And not even a mention of the murder in his letter?" I nearly cursed the man as an eccentric old fool. "What am I to do now?" I wondered dismally. The ride was a slow one. I had no desire to push my poor horse who was still recovering from the hurried trip into town, and my somber mood did not lend itself to anything but a dawdling gait anyway.

I was about halfway to The Copper Beeches when a bizarre climatic change occurred. The last rays of sunlight had just dipped behind the mountains when a cool, clammy mist began to descend on the valley. The temperature suddenly dropped thirty degrees. When I left for Fincastle the mercury had registered about eighty, and my attire was appropriate for that climate, but the abrupt decline now brought shivers down my spine.

As Ajax slowly plodded down the road, the mist grew thicker. Visibility quickly diminished to such a degree that I was glad that my horse seemed to instinctively know his way home. This strange fog that now blanketed the valley appeared not only to have neutralized the sense of sight, but that of hearing as well. The eerie mist seemed to absorb sound itself. The only noise audible was the monotonous clip of Ajax's hooves.

The professor's departure and this odd atmospheric change dominated my mind for most of the trip home. However, as I headed down our plantation's drive my mind abruptly returned to the problem at hand. What was I to do about Mr. Janus's murderer? In the last few months my steps toward manhood had been made in long strides. I decided that I would now complete the journey with one great leap.

The lights of our house slowly became visible through the mist. However it was not until I was ten feet from the front steps that I could see the structure itself. With great difficulty I guided

175

Ajax to the barn and stabled him. I removed the saddle and placed it on its stand. I opened the saddlebag and withdrew the pistol.

Lighting a lantern, I began walking toward the village. I was nervous, but I buried my trepidation deep within my chest. I was afraid not only of what would happen when I confronted the murderer, but also by what I might be forced to do. I had of course already concluded that fear was a useless emotion that served no purpose but to cloud perception and inhibit action, however this concept now proved easier in proclamation than in practice.

I could see no more than a few feet in front of me as I carefully made my way down the path. It was peculiar, but all was still dead silent. I had never before, or since, experienced a summer night without so much as a cricket's chirp. Gradually the grove of maples and pines loomed out of the mist. As I circumnavigated this company of silent sentinels, a few dim lights glowed through the dank shroud.

I entered the village and nearly ran into the wagon, and its contents gave me a start. The bloody cadaver of the mule lay mutilated in the bed. Its dead eyes stared up at me and the putrid smell of spilled blood wafted through the exposed ribcage. I approached the cabin's door, paused, and drew a deep breath of the night's murky vapor into my lungs. I knocked three times with the barrel of the gun.

The door swung open and I was greeted by the slave's smiling face.

"Oh! It you Massa Gid'in! Come on inside!" Ulysses welcomed me.

As I stepped in from the dark fog, the slave read the features of my face and saw the pistol in my hand. The grin fled his face and was replaced with an expression of somber panic. He fell back into one of the crude chairs that surrounded the table.

176

Penelope had her back to me when I entered, and as she turned and saw me, her facial features mutated much like those of her husband. Tears began to pour down her cheeks but she stood in silence.

I closed the door and took a seat at the table. I motioned for Penny to do the same, and she solemnly complied. I put the lantern on the floor and rested the gun on the table in front of me, though I kept my hand firmly upon it. We sat in silence for a moment. It was clearly my place to speak, but I found it difficult. Finally, I swallowed (I hoped imperceptibly) and addressed the couple.

"I know that Mr. Janus did not drown."

Ulysses merely stared at the floor.

"I also know that you killed him." I directed my comment to Ulysses.

Again the undeniably brave man sat motionless.

"I want you to tell me what happened."

The stoicism slowly faded and he looked over to his wife. She was still silently crying. She nodded to her husband and took his hand.

"Massa. Dare is someting sacred between a husban an his wife..." he broke off as a tear traced its way down his face.

He began again. "Penelope lef her Bible here on Sunday. Well, it ain't *her* Bible. You knows dat slaves can't have no books. It be Miss Janus' Bible."

I silently asked myself what Penny would possibly need a Bible for, but Ulysses answered my question as though he had read my mind.

"I bin teachin' Penelope to read."

"*You* know how to read?" I quietly asked, without betraying the slightest hint of emotion.

"Yas sir," he humbly replied.

"I found de Bible de other night and I knows dat if'n Miss Janus finds out dat it missin' she might never let Penelope come back to De Copper Beeches," he said as he affectionately looked into his wife's eyes.

"So," he continued, I lit out befo' sun up to git it back to her at Deep Dene. When I gits dare…" he stopped again. His muscles stiffened as though he were laboring to suppress a volcano of rage. "When I gits to her cabin I sees a candle lit. I looks in de window…When I sees him on top o' her…" He stopped again and gritted his teeth. "Dare is sometin' sacred between a husban an his wife…" he repeated his earlier statement nearly under his breath.

He looked hard into the fire that burned in the hearth, almost as an aside and said, "Massa. I know'd Penelope was hidin'somthin' from me all dis time. She never tell me doe. I tink she know I could never stand it… But she had no choice when he always be comin' to her cabin. What else could she do?" he posed the question more to himself than to me.

Shaking off his digression he returned to his story. "I fell down next to de door. I didn't know what to do. I jus' starts sobbin'. When dat man come out I grabs a rock and smashes him in de head." After making the gruesome confession, Ulysses stared off through the window into the impenetrable night, off into infinity.

"You then carried him to the pond and dumped him in?" I gently asked.

He nodded silently.

"When did you launch the boat?"

"Boat?" he blinked back to consciousness.

"After he leave, I put de fishin' pole in de boat an push it off," Penelope broke in.

"Did Mrs. Janus know what her husband had been doing?" I asked Penelope.

"She quietly nodded with downcast eyes. "I 's pretty sure. She never say anyting. But she kind to me anyways. I tinks she

178

knows it weren't me. I tinks she know it was her husban's fault."

I thought to myself for a moment. I surmised that Mrs. Janus would have preferred to sell Penelope off long before now, but her husband undoubtedly stood in the way. Even if she did not hold Penny responsible, I'm sure that her presence left an acerbic taste in the mouth of the mistress of Deep Dene.

Ulysses next did something that slaves rarely dared to do to a white man; he looked me straight in the eye. "Massa," he said. "I was in de barn de day of dat awful storm... I know'd what you bin readin'. I knows you a good man..." His tone was not one of contrition nor pleading for pity. It was a tone of admiration.

My mind spun back to that day, the day I fled the storm with such haste that I left the abolitionist literature in my saddlebags. I remembered when I recovered them; they seemed a bit out of sorts.

He paused for a second and took a deep breath. "Yas, I killed Janus. Afer what he bin doin' to my wife I killed him. Dares dem dat will have me strung up fo' dat. But If'n I was a White man, dem same people be fine wit what I done."

All was silent. I looked at the couple as they held hands, resigned to their fortune. We sat in silence for several minutes. I'm sure that the time ticked by mercilessly slowly for the couple, and I did not take the situation lightly. But I had to think things through before I acted. Eventually I stood, gun in hand, and they followed suit by standing as well. I looked the man straight in the eye. "It is terrible what happened to Mr. Janus..." Ulysses stood erect and thrust his chest out, ready to accept his fate. "...I hear drowning is an awful way to die."

I deposited the pistol in my belt and picked up the lantern. I walked to the door and turned to find the couple in each other's embrace. As their gaze met my own, I raised my forefinger to

179

my lips. They nodded their agreement to my unspoken instruction. I closed the door behind me as I left.

I re-entered the night to find that the fog was gone. Miraculously the air had cleared and a canopy of stars shone brightly overhead. The night had warmed and the symphony of insects had returned. A whip-or-will's call echoed through the darkness. As I meandered past the grove of maples and pines my lantern was made unnecessary by the bright yellow moon that was rising out of the trees.

It was not long after that fateful night that I began to formulate my plans, though it took a decade to bring them to fruition. The War Between the States of course began in '61 and Virginia seceded in April of that year. While Winston Jeffers and many of the other young men of Botetourt County rushed off to enlist, I was spared the call due to my uncle's failing health. In May the westernmost counties of Virginia, those on the other side of the Allegheny Mountains, voted to remain loyal to the Union. In June they organized a provisional government and in November they drew up a constitution. In December of '62 President Lincoln signed the Act of Admission and at present it looks as though the State of West Virginia will become a reality in less than a month.

Uncle Robert died in the winter of '62, leaving me as the sole proprietor of The Copper Beeches. I mourned the loss of my uncle, but by the time he expired, his affliction had transformed the once jovial man into a bedridden withered shell. However, the man I knew and loved had perished long before.

After my uncle passed, it did not take me long to execute my plan. With great sorrow I sold our ancestral home. I packed up all of our possessions and all of our people and left Botetourt County. I was purposefully vague when I told our neighbors that I planned on joining the army, and that I was moving my family to a "safer location." Taken literally, I was telling the truth. I purchased a sizable tract of land approximately 35 miles due

180

west of Fincastle. The farm was located in the heart of the anti-secessionist area and since Generals McClelland and Rosecrans had driven all Confederate forces from the region; it was indeed a safe place for my family. I freed every last one of our people and allowed any of our *former* slaves to remain as tenant farmers if they chose to do so. I had also been sincere in my intentions to join the army, though I doubt my neighbors would have approved of the color I elected to where. I applied for, and was granted, a commission in the 4th West Virginia Infantry, which is how I have found myself here, fighting under General Grant at the siege of the Confederate stronghold of Vicksburg.

The last letter I received from my cousin Eliza stated unsurprisingly that Bartholomew was managing the farm quite well in my absence. Ulysses, Penny, and their three children were doing well, as were the rest of our friends (former slaves) though Zeke had left the farm to join a colored regiment that had formed in New York.

I had heard from the professor once he reached Europe. His letter was a welcome, and much anticipated event. He related an interesting description of his Atlantic crossing, and he made an unusually subtle inquiry about the conclusion of my adventure. I responded at length, giving him an account of all that had transpired. I waited several months for a reply, but none ever arrived. I rewrote the letter and posted it again, but no response ever came. I even wrote to the University of Virginia, but the school responded that the professor was no longer affiliated with the institution. I often wondered what became of my mentor. I have vowed to pursue an explanation to that question if I survive this war.

So, as I conclude this narrative I hope I have answered any questions that may have arisen regarding my peculiar actions back in '62; as the apparently abrupt move from The Copper Beeches to West Virginia was not really abrupt at all. Nor was my decision to free our slaves or join the Union army. For you see, the origin of these actions lay in the events that had transpired more than a decade earlier; during that fateful summer when my principles began to evolve-- an evolution that culminated that misty night in the shadow of the maples and pines.